# McCURDLE'S ARM

## ANDREW FORBES

# McCURDLE'S ARM

## ANDREW FORBES

Invisible Publishing
Halifax | Fredericton | Picton

Library and Archives Canada Cataloguing in Publication
Title: McCurdle's arm : a fiction / Andrew Forbes.
Names: Forbes, Andrew, 1976- author.
Identifiers: Canadiana (print) 20240368835
            Canadiana (ebook) 2024036886X
            ISBN 9781778430565 (softcover)
            ISBN 9781778430572 (EPUB)
Subjects: LCGFT: Novels.
Classification: LCC PS8611.O7213 M33 2024 | DDC C813/.6—dc23

Edited by Bryan Ibeas
Cover and interior design by Megan Fildes
Typeset in Laurentian | With thanks to type designer Rod McDonald

Invisible Publishing is committed to protecting our natural environment. As part of our efforts, both the cover and interior of this book are printed on acid-free 100% post-consumer recycled fibres.

Printed and bound in Canada.

Invisible Publishing | Halifax, Fredericton, & Picton
www.invisiblepublishing.com

Published with the generous assistance of the Canada Council for the Arts, the Ontario Arts Council, and the Government of Canada.

 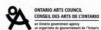 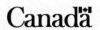

For CC

MCCURDLE'S FRONT TEETH were in the back of his throat. They'd been sent rattling back there by a smoker that'd flown up and in on him. He'd tracked it fine emerging from the pitcher's hand until sunlight danced off some lustred surface beyond centre field and the orb went from visible to invisible as though a sash had been pulled down before his eyes. Then the godawful impact, like a kicking horse. He sprawled in the dust, staring up at the tranquil blue sky.

Get up, ya fuckin mick, yelled a voice, hoarse, which might have been that of Henslow, the stately manager. Or not. Henslow tended to be more articulate in his upbraiding. A crank then, full of beer and whisky and heat stroke. There were brawls beneath the grandstand on a regular basis, kindled to flame by old-world sectarian animosities. Catholics took the brunt of it, and lord help you if your skin contained pigment (but then what in the hell would you be doing at the Quaker Grounds in Ashburnham on a Saturday afternoon in summer?).

McCurdle felt the blood pooling in his throat, coughed, rolled onto his flank, and expectorated a slimy red slug into the dirt, then one of his teeth. He reached up and fished out another with his fingers, held it in his fist as he slowly rose to stand bent with his hands on his knees, waiting for his equilibrium to return. In the swirl and murk behind his eyelids he saw in a flash the soft, fair face of Maureen, dark eyed and provoked with colour in her cheeks and lips, imagined running the back of his right hand against the skin of her thigh.

Do you wish to continue, McCurdle? asked the umpire, Feeney.

Fine, I'm fine, he said.

Then you may take your base, said Feeney.

Tooth in hand, McCurdle did so at a trot, slow and slightly meandering. By the time he stood at the bag, the stars had more or less dissipated. He spat a curt greeting to the Maroons' first baseman. Afternoon, Heese.

Shove it, mick. Wish he'd put it further down your Christing throat and you'd choked on it.

Scots.

What's that?

Family name's Scottish, not Irish.

Who in the shit cares? said the oafish first sacker, whose lips were crusted with dried sores glazed in tobacco juice.

McCurdle took his lead, three long sideways strides up the baseline.

The left handed–hitting Davis followed in the lineup. He stood in now, tall and lean, wagging his preferred forty-inch stick behind his ear as the Maroons' hurler collected himself.

The bowler now held the ball with both hands just below his chin. He snuck a peek over his shoulder to first. McCurdle smiled at him, leaned forward and collected a handful of dirt in the fist where his loosed incisor was still tucked. The most blistering heat the June sun could produce beat down on his neck and shoulders. A sour little breeze puffed over the grounds and all assembled there, then surrendered. Heese, said McCurdle, you'd better tell your boy I'm going.

The hell you are. You're still hearing bells.

All the same, McCurdle said, you smell like a Christing open latrine, and I'd just as soon put ninety feet between us.

I'd like to see it, Heese said.

Sure thing, Heese, McCurdle said, anything for you, and then broke for second, elbows churning, head down, knees driving.

Man's going, shouted Heese. McCurdle didn't allow himself a look until he was a few paces from where he'd need to begin his slide, if he were to take one. He saw the second baseman, Riley, once a teammate somewhere or other, racing in to take the catcher's throw, and as McCurdle dropped to the earth, he shot his right arm forward and flung open his tobacco-browned fingers, hurling his fist's contents toward Riley's face. Dirt clouded the defender's eyes, and the tooth bounced off his cheek. Riley blinked enough that the ball sailed through the space between his ear and his gloved left hand. It landed softly in the grass beyond, where the Maroons' homuncular yet speedy centre fielder loped over and collected it, tossing it back in to the pitcher.

Runner is safe, shouted Feeney, and McCurdle straightened himself and began brushing the dirt from his uniform.

That's it, bellowed Henslow from the bench. Crack running, boy!

Henslow called them all boy and son. The creeping suspicion was that it'd begun as a matter of a manager imparting the appropriate air of impartiality toward his charges, but that more and more the old strategist simply couldn't recall anyone's name. He'd shown up to a game without his teeth a few weeks back, had to send a bat boy running to his home several blocks distant, and just managed to gum his way through the exchange of lineup cards and the reminder of the ground's rules before the breathless child returned a scant moment before first pitch.

McCurdle advanced to third on a sacrifice push up the first-base line by Poppel, but Lehmann and Black both let third strikes go by, and the inning ended with him still standing there and no runs across for the Pine Groves. McCurdle grumbled, spat another sluice of blood and jogged out to centre, where his padded left-hand work glove remained as he'd left it in the shaggy grass.

It remained a wickedly hot and cloudless afternoon until the last half of the sixth inning, whereupon a thunderhead reared up from the western horizon, shook its mane, bore down on the field. The rain frilled out before it, an apron of sharp, stinging drops that advanced across the flat expanse of the outfield like the hem of a gown. Feeney let the contest continue for another half inning as spectators scrambled and puddles collected in the batter's box and in a pan-shaped depression behind second base before waving his hands over his head, signalling the match's suspension.

As McCurdle's fellow fielders sprinted from the meadow toward cover he stood probing the new interdental void with his tongue. He felt the thick wool of his uniform sponging rainwater and watched a stream of it cascade off his little finger. The rain was warm, but he could feel the chill as the breeze rushed over him. A thousand miles from home, a million miles from Maureen, a stringy, pulpy vacancy where his front teeth once sat. Flybitten, sunburned, the skin of his feet ragged. The muscles of his right shoulder and elbow inelastic and broadcasting a high, screeching pain two days out of three, and numbness in his last two fingers always. Three more months of this, and how many years after that.

He assumed these summers would one day be what killed him.

McCurdle was birthed in the tobacco fields around Ostrander and had been let out as a picker-for-hire, the family business, at ten. By noon the first day he knew it wasn't a life he wanted, had the childish audacity to imagine that something else might be possible.

On the long walk home, trailing his father, he threw stones at fenceposts and hit nine out of ten, and every day of his life thereafter he remembered the thrill of it—and also remembered thinking that it was maybe something he could do, and that if it promised to pull him out of the dirt of southwestern Ontario, he'd follow it as long as he could.

By thirteen he was playing with men and holding his own, though the barbs he received about his boniness and his smooth cheeks and his virginity (presumed, correctly) were savage. He learned how not to hear. He stretched out that winter, his shoulders solidifying, his voice dropping an octave. Come May next, several of the fieldhands on the team were unable to recognize him. One more season there, he figured, and then he'd try his hand in Detroit and perhaps the Wolverines would enlist him, which was pie-in-the-sky thinking but honest hope for a boy of his age.

But his mother fell ill in June, circling into a wicked delirium, the fever gripping her so tightly that the skin of her scalp felt as though it would split right open, or so she said. She laid up in McCurdle's bed, pushing him to the kitchen floor with a ragged blanket and a bundle of malodorous rags wrapped in burlap for a pillow.

As there were no women around, and McCurdle's father required a full night to recover from his daily labours as well as his nightly imbibing sessions, and McCurdle's older brother was two years gone on the Canadian Pacific (and had had his left leg mangled by an accident thereon, caught unawares when a car full of timber began to roll, though the family had not yet received word and would never see him again), the boy was put to work feeding and watering his mother. He carried dishes into the foul-smelling room, tried to find his gentle way out of her repeating conversations, emptied the pan, and changed the clothes of her bed and her body. He played no more base-ball that year, and when she passed away in October, the end was such guilty relief for him. They buried her quickly, before the snows came, in the Presbyterian cemetery next to McCurdle's still-born brother, Abraham, who was four years younger than him, or would have been.

McCurdle's father had always been a tippler, but he began drinking even more in order to marinate in his grief and expound loudly and wetly on his monumental misfortune. That winter was harried and treacherous, with McCurdle suffering many blows and black eyes. By March he was a young man, now nearly as tall as his father and broader across the chest. He understood there'd be no use in asking the old man if he might be allowed to continue to play ball, so he woke before the sun one harsh morning as the wind scoured the crusts of snow yet lying in shadows and low places, packed his glove and spikes in a flour sack, and began walking west. He made St. Thomas by the dinner hour and wandered the puddled streets, suddenly realizing that he'd no idea what to do now that he'd wrestled his freedom. He was helpless as a robin.

When full darkness came, he hopped a US-bound freighter and, fearing the wrath of American authorities, leapt off in Windsor. He slept in a Lutheran cemetery for six nights before finding a shift at the Grand Trunk depot unloading empty green glass bottles, brand new and blown at

Mallorytown, temporarily taking the place of a man who'd gone missing. A foreman recommended a rooming house and loaned him enough for his first night of sleeping in a real bed somewhere other than his family's home. Young McCurdle filled in the rest of the week for this missing man, and as the man had not returned by the following Monday the position was his. He worked without complaint or pause and eventually earned employment with the Hiram Walker company, sweeping the distillery's grain warehouse. When the lilac began to show that May he found himself on the company team.

McCurdle played wherever they needed him. His assets were his great speed and a tremendous right arm. When tasked with hurling he commanded the box with his whistling fireball and a crafty self-taught looper.

The Walkers were the cream of the Industrial League, farm boys who, like McCurdle, had moved to town to lift and push things for pay, and who could to a man swing the bats and pitch the pill with ferocious acumen. They played late on Thursday and Friday afternoons, doubleheaders on Saturday, then wandered out of the city guzzling liquor from those selfsame glass bottles, shitting in ditches, braying at the moon, collapsing in the fields. On Sunday mornings they were pious, resting their bodies and laundering their souls in preparation for the befoulings of the week ahead.

With his mother lying in the shady Ostrander churchyard and his father estranged, McCurdle was without question alone and solely responsible for making his way in the world. Now, with regular pay and extra income from his success on the ballfield, he was set in his course, an itinerant labourer of general skill who could help make a winner of a company ballclub.

He was thus employed, variedly but consistently, from his fifteenth year right up through his lengthy Pine Grove stint when, as a veteran of twenty-three seasons—from Windsor to Brockville, New York State to one desperate, broiling, drunken summer in Oaxaca—he'd patched together what he supposed one might call a living, or even a life.

All of it, though, was in service to the stubborn dream of marrying his dark-haired love, Maureen Chatwin.

She'd sprung from a place called Oxford Station, which as she described it was nothing but a singletrack rail station surrounded by fields of rocks in the unremarkable flat scrub of far eastern Ontario. Spindly cedar trees and hefty black flies, she said. It wasn't readily apparent what had inspired the decision to place the station there, forty miles south of Ottawa and twenty north of the St. Lawrence River. It made precious little sense. She said the curious placement of the depot and the hamlet that had sprung up around it almost certainly had affected her outlook on the world. Born into nonsense, she said, good luck finding your way to good sense. Her self-deprecations seemed precision-machined to intoxicate him.

A schoolteacher herself, she was one of four daughters of Angus Temple Chatwin—a grocer and merchant, devout Anglican, and widower, who taught his daughters rigorous self-discipline and respect for the written word as well as the Word of God. Young Maureen had eventually found a position in Brockville as headmistress of a two-room schoolhouse that featured electric heat, the latter a gift from a wealthy family whose slow-witted boy had benefited from Maureen's patient tutorage. Despite the school having adopted the Chautauqua system and consequently closing for the summer holiday in July and August, she remained ever present with the doors unlocked for tutoring, determined as she was that those in her charge should enjoy the fuller experience of the world that one only realizes through complete literacy. She was also kept busy leading Sunday school lessons in the basement of the Methodist assembly hall. Though her calendar featured no break, she found her relaxation watching sport, with base-ball her most ardent passion, as her father had been an adherent and taught her its nuance and appreciation. His only caution had been that she resist the temptation to wager on the outcomes of games, as such activity would endanger her soul.

McCurdle passed three seasons in Brockville with Staley's Vireos, resplendent in their fine buff-coloured stockings, and though he'd certainly noted Maureen on several occasions, it wasn't until his final campaign there that he first spoke to her. It was a perfect Saturday afternoon in July, and she was installed in her usual box seat, unaccompanied and in a broad straw hat with a ribbon in the same soft shade of brown as the players' uniforms. He commented on this to her as he awaited his turn at the dish, clutching four bats in his great hands and swinging them in wide circles.

I'm a great supporter, she said.

I admire your devotion.

And I admire your skill, she declared.

He saw then the smile she failed to hide, tinged with mischief, affection, and tenderness at once, and the possibility, if the world spun only a little differently, of a wild and tumultuous affair. That was enough for him. It was then, it was now, and it always would be.

They were matched from the outset and pledged themselves to one another shortly thereafter, but her stipulations were firm: she'd be his only once he'd settled into place and abandoned the peripatetic life to which he'd become

9

accustomed, and which his ballplaying necessitated, semi-professional clubs and leagues being something less than permanent in nature. In McCurdle's mind this meant at last catching on with a prestigious professional outfit—in the National League, ideally—whereas for Maureen the obvious implication was that he would abandon the game, find a trade, and earn a dependable living that enabled him to buy a spacious house, which they would together endeavour to fill with babies.

To her considerable credit, she had not placed a limitation of time on said stipulation and did not waste effort in attempts to get McCurdle to accelerate his own epiphany, but remained steadfast and patient while he traipsed the continent plying his craft. He thought of her always, and was likewise loyal in both body and soul, but pressed on ever as though just one more semi-professional season—splitting time between slashing across third-rate diamonds and performing backbreaking yet thoughtless jobs in backwater towns—would succeed in catching the attention of a proball potentate such as Harry Von der Horst in Baltimore or Chris von der Ahe in in St. Louis. McCurdle had read about these men in barbershop sporting papers, and oftentimes daydreamed that one of them would send for him, pencil him into the lineup, and collect the gate receipts as the pitcher-and-slugger became a headline-grabbing sensation.

It might require mention that McCurdle had been remarkably if briefly handsome, specifically in the interval of time after his shoulders had filled out and his skin cleared and before the sun and wind and dust and collisions with catchers and beanings both accidental and otherwise had scored and weathered his face to shoe leather, the tobacco had darkened his teeth, and his nose and jaw had become knotted and lumpy. And now the missing teeth. It was his great fortune that Maureen first knew him in that short spell when he was still fresh and pink, his fair reddish hair thick and full and reaching before his ears and down his jaw, where terminated two formidable chops. His joints were loose and painless. He was doubly lucky that that was apparently what she still saw when gazing upon him. She'd formed an image and it stuck. If he were to meet her for the first time now she'd overlook him completely or turn and run for the hills, he was certain.

They caught the boy who'd blinded McCurdle from beyond centre field. A couple of the boys, namely Harry Black and Bon Lehmann, intercepted word of a scheme hatched by the Maroons' travelling supporters involving a silver dish and a young man of sixteen or so stationed beyond the high outfield wall. In fact he'd been up a tree there, attempting to redirect rays of sunlight into Pine Grove batters' eyes. The transgressor had been haphazard in his aim until McCurdle's fateful trip to the plate when he'd managed to align his platter in such a position as to provide the flash that made that sailing fastball disappear from McCurdle's vision just long enough to put him in harm's way, thus endangering his smile. Black and Lehmann interrogated Maroon boosters until one of the latter group admitted to having heard of the plan, and the two Pine Groves chased a rumour into Michael Potter's Inn, where more of the out-of-towners were dining. It took only the unspoken threat of physical violence by Lehmann's intimidating person for the Marooners to surrender a name. Thus did Jacob Robert

11

Wheeler very suddenly become the most wanted man in Ashburnham.

Without considerable trouble they found him cowering behind a crate of eggs at the station, pitifully abandoned by his fellow boosters, the high-polished silver dish still tucked under his arm, his too-large bowler pulled over his eyes, waiting for the evening train back to Toronto. This must be Wheeler, said Black, hauling the boy so firmly by the arm that the lad's shoulder slid from its socket. The youth gave a trailing whimper that suggested that his faculties had already begun to leave him, which in all likelihood would prove a small blessing in the face of what was soon to come.

At this very same moment McCurdle was likewise in a compromised state. Once the rain had lifted he had been sent off to a denturist across the river to be fitted for porcelain teeth, and he was still there, in a reclining chair and quite numb on powerful overproof whisky. The denturist, his brow dripping, had discovered in McCurdle's jaw some remnant of one of the missing teeth, and before probing with his sharpest tool in hopes of effecting an extraction of this shard he'd poured a great glass of his own home-stilled spirit over the ravaged gum and down the ballplayer's throat. The denturist busied himself about the room, waiting for the athlete's faculties to blunt, at which point he planned to excavate around in the man's mouth, widen the laceration where the teeth had been, clamp down on the fragment with locking pliers and begin to yank. His concern was that, even inebriated to the point of incapacitation, the solidly built McCurdle would require restraint for his arms and legs.

The denturist had only just said I'd kindly now ask that you count from seventy-nine to seventy in reverse fashion and McCurdle had begun to attempt the trick when Black flung open the door and said, We found the little shitfucker, McCurdle.

You did what? said McCurdle with rubber lips around an insensate tongue.

Please, we're not to be interrupted here. Mr. McCurdle requires surgical intervention.

You found what? Cross-eyed and still in his uniform.

The hog-bastard boy that blinded you. Lehmann's got him and we're going to pulp him, but we figured it only fair that you had a chance to contribute.

McCurdle was descending into a cave beneath a very large mountain and could only barely hear the echoes of the voices of those speaking, but he thought he made out well enough what was being said. Well, sure, he said, if it needs to be done. So over the denturist's protests he stood unsteadily, which caused the practitioner to wish he'd utilized the restraints immediately. McCurdle lurched after Black out the door and into the late day sunlight bathing the dusty street and very shortly they encountered Lehmann, who'd been making his way toward the denturist's office. Lehmann had Wheeler slung over his shoulder like a lamb. The boy was bruised about the face in a manner to suggest he'd recently and ill-advisedly objected to being carried in such a fashion.

McCurdle, thank Christ, said Lehmann. He flung the boy down to the ground, where the latter landed awkwardly on his damaged shoulder, then rolled halfway over and found himself squinting into the sinking sun. He offered no words, only the faintest of peeps.

Black landed an enthusiastic boot into the young Torontonian's groin, which reddened the prone fellow's face. Have a swing, McCurdle, said Black, and McCurdle attempted to do so but missed wide with a slow kick and nearly upset himself. Another, said Black, but McCurdle had become quite dizzy and put his hands on his knees to steady himself.

Here, said Lehmann, let me, and he swung an enormous black preacher boot, his right, toward Wheeler's jaw. Wheeler saw it coming and reacted, though he still caught it in the forehead. The impact made a clopping sound like a hoof on packed earth. Wheeler fell back with his eyes closed and a large red welt formed above his brow as he lay still and quite unconscious.

Well shit, he's quit on us, said Black.

One more, said Lehmann. McCurdle? But McCurdle only murmured and allowed a thin dribble to fall from his lips into the dust at his feet.

All right, said Lehmann, for McCurdle, and then popped the inert youth once more in the ear. The denturist emerged just then from his door and took McCurdle by the shoulders and led him back inside. Lehmann said, See you at the yard, McCurdle, and then Lehmann and Black dispersed and the Wheeler boy was carried to the police house, where he spent the night. In the morning he was put on the train, his head and shoulder alight with pain, and it was suggested to him that he might never be welcome in Ashburnham again.

McCurdle fell asleep in the denturist's chair, and when he came around the procedure had been successful. Once his head cleared some he stood and put on his coat and hat and went out into the evening, his lip packed with gauze. He'd had impressions taken for false teeth, which would be ready in a matter of days. The Pine Grove supporters' club took up a collection to pay for McCurdle's new smile in full, and by the following weekend our man stood on the mound and waved to the crowd, merrily showing it off before dusting the Astonishers, surrendering no runs while tripling in two himself in a tidy 5–0 victory.

The Quaker Grounds rested in the lea of a wrought-iron truss bridge that spanned the Whetung River. The covered wooden grandstand had been erected on six acres of land belonging to the one-time lumber baron turned brewer Spencer Grafton, who not so coincidentally also owned the Pine Groves base-ball club. The first-base grandstand ran parallel to the river, and the outfield fence of splintery eight-foot pine boards ran in a clean arc from the southwest corner of the lot to the northeast, where it was abutted by the outer wall of a fine if not terrifically spacious clubhouse. Early in the season, in April worst of all, the runoff and the rains would engorge the Whetung and the water would seep beneath the grandstand and make a swamp of the visitors' bench and the first-base area. Those seated in the last two or three rows along the first-base line could feel the mist and spray on their necks and hear the roar, the river alive like the braiding of muscle.

The Pine Groves were turned out in rich cream-coloured suits of heavy wool flannel with the letters P and G chain-stitched across the chest in heavy forest-green threading. The flat-topped cream caps bore green felt on the brim and two courses of shining ribbon around the crown. McCurdle was fond of the stockings, in matching green, and so pleasingly tight that they stayed high without sagging and made his calves ripple and bulge like a thoroughbred at full gallop. He liked the way he looked and felt in the uniform.

Experience told him that the material would weather and age, such that by August the cream wool would be stained brown and grey, with small red polka dots where he'd killed the blood-full insects that plagued the fielders in the worst of the summer's heat. The stockings would stretch and droop. The cap would lose its stiffness and a crescent of darkness would spread out across where it sopped the sweat of his forehead. Some of the ribbon would pull or tear. There'd be gouges and holes in the britches. He usually wore through two to three pairs of spikes in a campaign. When times were good and his foresight intact he'd keep back part of his first pay of the new season to purchase an auxiliary set to hold in reserve for the inevitable afternoon when the right sole would begin to flap loose, or the toe of his left punched clean through by another player's spike. He'd have them repaired if possible, but that took time, and he wasn't about to miss action for want of footwear. That was precisely the sort of scenario that was likely to permit a beardless boy to drop into your spot and show some flash, bumping you to the end of the bench, a short step away from earning your outright release.

It was a difficult way to earn pay but he'd seen enough of the alternatives to know he preferred this one. People who came from where he came from didn't generally aspire to more. He'd suffer the pain as long as he could, and what came after was a terrifying unknown he preferred not to consider while dry.

The Pine Groves saw to the needs of their bodies as they perceived them. Sleep, liniment, drink, sex. Sausage and whisky, potatoes. Pungent medicinal pastes applied thickly, wrapped beneath cotton strips. Some of the men—Hewitt, Black, and Cook—were married and kept their wives close.

It was public knowledge that the catcher Long Tom Klopp kept the frequent company of night women, though those in the fraternity saw no harm in it as long as he employed the sheepskin, which his continued good health suggested he did. His wife was by all accounts blind to his recreations.

Drink was nearly a second vocation for the men, behind ballplaying and ahead of regular work. They celebrated every win and each marvellous play, keeping a list of them in their minds so that there was always a reason to raise their mugs. Grafton often rewarded his players' efforts with cases of ale, and there were several good establishments in Ashburnham, Potter's being a favourite, as well as a good music hall that would not underserve a patron with coins in his pocket. Mc-Curdle once had such an unbridled evening there that he forgot how his legs worked and had to be carried to his rooming house on the back of a stout hog butcher.

There was a generally festive air when the Pine Groves gathered to drink, though in McCurdle's case the reasons for such heroic intake of spirits were typically less Dionysian and more in pursuit of abnegation of the self. He hurt fervently for Maureen, and in the same breath he suffered torment each moment he was not suited up and playing ball. Distillate of grain made such things seem more distant for a few blessed hours.

When sober the Ashburnham players were an impressive group, though coarse and occasionally cretinous, and as with any collection of men, not without their peculiarities. The Kincardine twins, identical to their blemishes, and who played excellent infield at short and third (interchangeably, Henslow believed, erroneously), spoke low to one another in language indecipherable to others, which spooked some of their fellow Pine Groves. Poppel sprayed like a hydrant whilst shouting, which he frequently did. Keenan smoked a foul-smelling pipe when seated on the bench.

Stroud was an amateur botanist who had to be watched when stationed in the outfield lest he discover while on patrol a patch of wildflowers he determined to be of particular note. Once when responsible for left field he chased a towering fly ball into foul territory and looked to have a play on it, but stopped short in his pursuit because there on the gentle slope toward a creek stood a clump of dainty columbines that he daren't trample. The ball fell harmlessly, the striker's life extended. When questioned on it once back to the bench, he told Henslow, Cap, there was the fattest bumblebee climbing up, right up, you understand, into the purple bell of the flowers, and who am I to interfere in such a timeless natural process as pollination? He was a headache, but his bat couldn't be denied, so his spot on the squad was secure.

Nature often intruded on their playing surfaces, given the quality of the fields available to teams in the South Western Ontario Base-Ball Players' Association. There was a patch of poison ivy harassing fielders in the deepest right corner of the Astonishers' grounds, and a wicked thatch of wild raspberry stood ready to thrash the arms of unsuspecting combatants in the farthest reach of the Silver Stars' park. When tramping the latter, the wise went in spikes first, fished around for the ball and knocked it out with a toe.

Nor was it exclusively plant life. One afternoon in Petawawa, where McCurdle played a year in the Lumbermen's circuit, he stood in the pasture amid ten or a dozen cackling geese with two men on base, and when the ball was struck past him, the wretched birds hissed and jabbed so furiously the beaks at the ends of their serpents' necks that he had to give up the chase, allowing the batter to round the bases while McCurdle stood with his hands in the air apologetically. The runs proved the difference, as the Mattawas prevailed. Later the Gaulish third baseman, who had barely any English, told him he'd have carved his way through the birds, and then produced from the waist of his trousers a horrible-looking blade. Made in Meheeco, he said, and McCurdle spent some time that evening wondering if the dried blood thereupon had been avian or human in provenance.

On another occasion, when he'd hopped the border to play for Potsdam of the Empire Association, he chased down a ball rolling over the uneven terrain of the Cheektowaga outfield only to watch a red fox, its coat lustrous as shellac, dart into a hole—followed by the ball, which rolled into the very same cavity. He glanced at the field where the batsman was steaming around second, then tentatively extended his hand into the recess but recoiled when he felt the canid's hot breath on his knuckles. As it was the only decent ball between either club, the contest was called and no score recorded.

On his way out the door of his rooming house McCurdle bent to leave a saucer of milk for the ragged little cat with a lopsided face that frequently slunk about the front step there. He'd first seen it the very day he'd moved in, and that same evening he'd left it a sliver of fish on a scrap of oilcloth, to which it reacted with begrudging gratitude, and their relationship had continued that way steadily since. McCurdle had originally thought it might be missing an eye, but one day as it purred around his pantleg he wrapped his hand around its skull and held it firmly, though the animal was frantically struggling to free itself, and rubbed the eye-socket with his thumb to discover that the eye was present but the fur around it matted so that it appeared shut.

Presently the cat emerged from a dogwood shrub clumped roadside and gave a happy mew. It dashed for the dish he'd left it while McCurdle strode on down the street.

Meeting Long Tom at the barber shop as they'd arranged, McCurdle found Klopp freshly shorn and reading the *Recorder*. The barber's chair was empty, so McCurdle took a seat and asked for the usual. The barber caped him and began.

Here is McCurdle, Klopp read aloud. Excuse me, he said, you'll want to know the headline. It reads: PINE GROVES DRUB TECUMSEHS. The article then: Here is McCurdle, right on time. The hurler and patroller of the Quaker Grounds' spacious centre field lawn has begun to put it all together for the men in green this summer. McCurdle's arm is in top form, slipping the bean past eleven Tecumsehs in the first of two games this Saturday past, a 9–3 Ashburn-ham victory, and wielding a big stick, too, bringing across four runs with his three knocks. The big man is batting a mean .422 thus far this season and shows no signs of cool-ing off. The Groves—

That's good, said McCurdle, that's enough, as the barber trimmed his nape.

Klopp folded the *Recorder* down, looked over at McCur-dle reclined in the chair. Sure you don't want to hear more? he said. It gets good here.

No thanks, Kloppy. I think that's enough.

Impressive showing, said the barber. Highest average in the league.

Some league, said McCurdle, his mind at once in Detroit, New York, Chicago, and Brockville. Anywhere but where he was. To have found himself atop a very small mountain pleased him less each morning. He was running out of ways in which to forestall his senescence, and it soon would come calling, with him never having seen a pitch in the National League. Can a person call himself successful in such a circumstance?

Says you were born in Leamington, Klopp persisted. I didn't know that.

Wasn't. Come from a nothing little town nearby nobody's ever heard of. A crossroads.

Name of?

Ostrander.

I know it.

The hell you do.

Sure, on the road from Ingersoll to Tillsonburg, isn't it?

'Tis.

I was chased out of it once by an angry father, but I was only passing through anyway. One night only, like most of my appearances were in those days.

The barber, who was familiar with Klopp's reputation, only smiled as he worked.

Well, what do you know. Klopp was the closest thing to a chum McCurdle had on the Pine Groves, owing mostly to the similarity in their ages—Klopp just months younger—and similar tenures, McCurdle having latched on with the club only a month after Klopp began there, four years back now. They often drank together, and Mrs. Klopp would insist her husband invite McCurdle for a Sunday dinner two or three times a season. At these affairs McCurdle watched his words to avoid implicating his teammate in the unsavoury adventures everyone but Klopp's wife knew him to enjoy. It was tiring, though she made a good roast.

Always thought you were born in Windsor, said Klopp.

The barber scurried around, held up the mirror behind his head to suggest to McCurdle that he was done, so long as McCurdle approved. Everything looked even. He nodded.

McCurdle said, I was, in a manner of speaking.

It was clear this made little sense to Klopp but he chose not to pursue. Something else had his attention. Now hold on, he said. Says you could well be done after this year?

Says what?

McCurdle, Klopp quoted, who may not be renewed for the next championship season—

According to who?

Doesn't specify. Grafton? Have you spoken to our man Spence?

Not recently, nor with any measure of specificity. Who's written the article?

Welt.

Baxter Welt.

He has Grafton's confidence.

Does he.

Klopp said, In my estimation, yes.

McCurdle closed his eyes and thought about this. The barber was slapping his neck with the horsehair brush and unclipping the cape. McCurdle sat a moment longer in rumination while the barber stood and Klopp leaned, both men looking at him, waiting for him to speak.

How much longer did he have in him? It was the question he never fully faced, always turning away before any honest attempt at reckoning toward an answer. Playing, pushing, working, trying. The whole dread enterprise of living the way he did. Liquor, aches, worry, hecklers, fistfights, a ball in the mouth. The constant high-pitched refrain of his right arm's squeal, and the numbness further down. These men who were his peers, from lumber camps, railways, canoe works, iron foundries, farm fields. Louts and liars, giants and saints. They performed astonishing feats as well as acts of unfathomable cruelty, and though nothing ruins a base-baller's reputation quite like kindness, there persisted whisperings of great altruistic works conducted in confidence. How much longer would all of this suit, and how many more games did he have in him? Would he be done with the game before the game was done with him? Much as he wished to avoid such inquiry he felt in his blood that an accounting was soon due.

And perhaps that was all right. The image recurrent in his dreams was of waking in the early hours with dearest Maureen asleep next to him, an open window on a hot night, the softest cooling breeze light on his face, the feeling of being wrapped in the Earth's sweet benevolence. A thousand nights of this, ten thousand, adding up to something like grace.

Welt's probably just guessing, said McCurdle finally, then stood and brushed the front of his pantlegs, glanced once more at himself in the big mirror, and dug into his pocket for the right coin, which he laid on the walnut counter and walked out into the afternoon, which was thick with dust and pollen and heat.

How's your arm, McCurdle? shouted a man on the opposite side of the street. McCurdle simply raised his left and waved.

By the first week of June, after a month of play and one quarter of the season recorded, the Pine Groves had eleven victories, which trailed only the thirteen accrued by the Biltmores, whom they'd yet to face.

The Redstarts arrived from London on a wet, cool Thursday afternoon and proceeded from the station directly to the Quaker Grounds via three carriages. Grafton welcomed the visiting contestants imperiously while an aide held an umbrella over his head. The Redstarts' player–manager, a small, pinch-faced second baseman named Clarke, shook the old man's hand and then stood in the drizzle listening as Grafton expostulated. Clarke nodded, wriggled his moustache, clasped his hands behind his back, and when finally released by Grafton with a second handshake, jogged over to his players and huddled with them.

Tall, thin Henslow watched all this while seated in the final row of the covered first-base grandstand, occasionally looking down at the two lineup cards he'd already filled out, one set on each knee. On the card balanced on his left knee, McCurdle was listed as the starting pitcher and the third batter, while Cook played in centre and hit eighth. On the other card, perched on the manager's right, Poppel was named as pitcher, batting fifth; McCurdle played centre and batted in his customary third spot; and Cook sat.

Henslow reached into his coat pocket and removed his leather cigar case, unlatched it, and pulled out a panatela. He returned the case to his overgarment. On the field, near second, a young member of Finn Robinson's grounds crew was trying to use a rake to disperse a puddle. The rain had become a drizzle and was now perhaps only a mist. With luck it would let up and the afternoon's game would proceed unhindered.

Henslow chewed, spat, gently bit the cigar between his teeth and lit it with a match, then turned and dropped the spent match over the seatback and into the wet bushes there. He made it a habit to mind where he dropped a match because he'd seen too many wooden structures such as this go up more easily than a person might think possible. In his playing days he'd been in Trois-Rivières when the bank of tiered seating beyond third base had begun to smoke and light and then glow ominously. The spectators cleared out, but the game continued because dark was coming and the championship standings required that Shawinigan and Trois-Rivières complete the match. The umpire ruled *en français* that unless the conflagration or its smoke impeded play the match should continue. The wind carried the thick smoke off and away from the field. By the final inning the last third of the structure was in full flame such that Henslow could feel the heat on his right forearm and cheek from his post at shortstop. While his proximity to the flames was unsettling, it also provided enough light by which to track the ball, which proved helpful as the dusk gathered, and he himself watched the final out settle into his hands to deliver the home team its glory.

The grounds crew worker had moved on to a dip in short centre that tended to fill with rainwater. Another worker had emerged from the shed just beyond the home bench trundling a barrow full of sand that he was now steering toward the pitcher's box. The sky over the fence was lightening noticeably. The Redstarts had adjourned to the tavern immediately across the mud-filled road to graze over some food before game time. It was beginning to look as though they'd meet the intended three o'clock starting hour.

Henslow was aware of the talk and could only offer that he'd always been bad with names. Lately, though, he'd noticed a greater inability to link a face to its referent. But the essential cognition remained sturdy. He could strategize, recognize talent, and build a lineup. Names weren't strictly necessary, not if they threatened to crowd out the important material.

The question currently before the respected and road-weary commodore was the health of his best player's arm. In his outing the previous Saturday, McCurdle had acquitted himself admirably, as noted by the local paper, but in the second game of the twin bill he'd come off the field from his post in centre after having chased down a rolling ball and heaved it toward second, complaining of a dead arm. The throw bounced twice before reaching Davis at the bag, unusual for McCurdle. When Henslow asked the veteran said, My arm's angered. It's got no electricity to it, Cap, he'd said. No jump. And my fingers are fiery, stabbing with pain.

Henslow had made a special trip to McCurdle's rooming house on Wednesday evening, bringing a box of Finister's tea for Mrs. Sullivan, the landlady. He knocked on McCurdle's door, went in, and said, I'm here to know about your arm. Is it good for tomorrow, or any time this stand?

And McCurdle had stood and said, I'll be fine to go, Cap, no concern there.

But Henslow knew that a man in McCurdle's position would say anything to ensure his continued role. McCurdle stood in the middle of his small room facing his manager, swinging his right arm over his head and in jerking circles to prove its fitness, curling the fingers into a fist and then splaying them out over and over again.

Well, we'll see, said Henslow to his second longest–tenured player. He said, Take it easy at the brewery tomorrow, and both men laughed, knowing how impossible that was likely to be. The majority of team owners saw their most treasured players' employment merely as pretext for their inclusion on the team, and so worked them very lightly, or anyway lighter than their non-playing peers. Not Grafton, who it sometimes seemed sought out the roughest, strongest ballplayers just to have workers capable of lifting greater loads over longer periods. Henslow thought that the owner was due a lesson in protecting one's investments.

Henslow had two options: he could bet on McCurdle to be well enough to win one or two games in this four-long stretch; or he could park him in the outfield for these matches, use him sparingly in the midterm, and save the arm for three weekends hence when the Pine Groves would travel to Guelph to challenge the Biltmores, where he could lean on the veteran for three or four of those matches.

Henslow puffed greyly, clouds into clouds. The boys had begun to show: Cook and Black strolled from the brewery up Baker Street and onto the grounds. He could see the Kincardines not far behind, ambling toward the clubhouse and conferring in their strange language. The umpire would be along soon. The crowd would gather—for it looked as though they'd have a game today—and the festivities would commence. Henslow needed a decision.

The manager puffed some more, and in time he tore up the card that had rested on his left knee. He'd seen a significant number of players of McCurdle's age and stature go into precipitous decline, and generally the story began like this: a pain in a joint, a prickling sensation.

He stood and made his way down the steps to the field and then toward the clubhouse in left field, where his players had begun to prepare for the game.

Kid Poppel's fast one was snapping, and his dropper was dipping. He had a wide crossbody delivery, his arm swooping low and his wrist whipping at the point of release, which imparted a fierce spin. When he felt the ball well—in his fingertips, and the palm of his hand—it did as he wished it to. On this day he felt the ball quite well.

It helped too that Kid was quite unashamedly loading it up with black tobacco spit and a thick mixture of petroleum jelly and beeswax that he reapplied each inning to the brim of his cap, as was standard practice. As the season was well underway most all of the balls they employed were darkened, resembling only in general shape the lovely objects they'd been in May, when Grafton's accounts man sent away for a fresh dozen of Albert G. Spalding's baseballs, clean and white as new pearls. They would dwindle in number, several lost in vegetation or the river's rush and others damaged beyond use, while those still existing would deteriorate in condition, gone soft as pillows and stained dark as midnight.

The Redstarts' first man chipped the third pitch of the game toward the middle of the diamond, where Tip Kincardine scooped it up but erred on the throw to Harry Black at first, putting the batter safely on. The second batter slashed at a burner and struck it weakly into the air in front of home plate, where Klopp was waiting for it. Poppel then induced the third striker to send a ball bounding through the pitcher's box toward second, where Davis fielded it, stepped on the bag, and whirled to deliver a perfect ball to Black, thereby ending the top of the inning.

Stroud reached on a hard slap toward left to begin the last half of the inning, and Tiny Kincardine followed with a walk, putting two men on for McCurdle, who stood swinging four bats over his shoulder and in quick circles behind his back as Tiny jogged up the line. McCurdle's elbow twinged only slightly as the bat heads looped away from his body, and not so much that he worried about his swing. He dropped the three extra bats and walked toward the box, where he corkscrewed the spikes of his right shoe into the ground. He liked to leave his lead foot free and unburdened. Then he looked across his left shoulder.

The pitcher was one he'd not seen before, dark haired and perhaps dusky. McCurdle had heard chatter that London had rostered a Cuban fellow, or possibly a Mohawk, and this might very well be that man. More importantly this pitcher had shown both Lehmann and Tiny a ferocious moving ball—it seemed to crest late and then dive toward the right—and so McCurdle was on hooks wondering how he'd recognize this pitch and how he'd react if he did.

He stood in and let two fast ones go by, the first near his eyebrows and the second lower and too far off the dish to reach. Then came the mover, and he recognized it as soon as it left the man's hand, for the Redstart's arm came over in a different place and his hand looked like a claw or a raven's foot. The ball proceeded straight for a time and then quite suddenly and clearly it veered, as though it'd hit a snag, and while once it had been on a path to take it over the heart of home plate, it now bore down on McCurdle's back foot. He flinched to see it.

It landed near the catcher's left shoe to settle in the soft dirt there, and the catcher bent at the waist and collected it with both hands, the right one bare and the other sporting its padded fingerless glove of the sort then gaining popularity. This catcher also had a kind of stuffed, reinforced singlet over his uniform to protect the abdomen, as well as cricket-style shin wrappings. Apart from his wire-frame mask, which most all backstops wore, the Redstart catcher's outfit stood out to McCurdle, who was accustomed to Kloppy's minimal suit of leather work gloves, truncated leather apron worn under his shirt, and magazines wrapping his shins beneath the stockings.

The London catcher zipped it back to the hurler while McCurdle tried to memorize the path the ball had taken.

Carney, the umpire, was slow to report. That, gentlemen, was a strike, he said at last.

Beg your pardon, said McCurdle. Look where it came to rest. He indicated the little crater with the tip of his bat.

Gauperie, Henslow shouted from the bench. Horsefeathers. Quite unsound.

But while airborne, said Carney, it penetrated the zone.

It would have to be a magic ball to do that.

I'd agree it was lively, said Carney, but that's my judgment.

Jesus, said McCurdle, how's a batter to defend against that?

On the next delivery McCurdle was watching for the darting ball again and was therefore caught flatfooted when it turned out to be a bullet, straight enough to hang laundry on and placed perfectly, moving the count to two balls and two strikes. As was his custom with a pair of marks against him, McCurdle next moved his hands a little further apart and a little higher up toward the barrel.

He expected another dipper and got it, coming in a touch slower but turning so quickly on its axis it seemed to hiss. He dropped his right foot back slightly and then took a short, choppy hack at the spot right in on his hands where he'd calculated the ball was likely to be. He felt the jab and then a jolt as he met it there, only an inch or three from his right index finger, but he'd gotten over top of the ball enough that it shot down to the spot in front of the plate the Pine Groves called the rock garden, a hardpacked area between home and the pitcher's box that Finn Robinson deliberately underwatered and into which he'd tamped a collection of small, flattish rocks he'd collected while wading in the river. The notion behind this bit of landscaping was that the home-side boys could beat a ball into the ground there and know it would be likely to bounce both high and at an irregular angle, surprising the pitcher and fielders and giving the Pine Grove runners and batter a chance to advance. Such inbuilt advantages were commonly employed by teams throughout the South West, and indeed across the base ball–playing world, so consequently the visitors might resent the advantage but did not protest it lest their own peculiar groundskeeping choices be subject to scrutiny.

McCurdle often executed this maneuver with intent, but in this case he'd merely been attempting to make some manner of contact in order to move Stroud and Tiny along. Once he saw where it was going and then watched it take a wild leap, he was off like a jackrabbit toward first. The pitcher moved in and stood looking up, waiting for the ball to come down, and when it settled in his hand he made a devil of a throw to first to nab McCurdle, at least in Carney's estimation. Bugger, shouted Henslow. Stroud and Tiny each moved up a station.

Joe Davis, whose proper given name was Josephus Catullus, was the sturdiest of the Pine Groves. The son of a well-read or perhaps over-read Lambton dairy farmer, Joe had begun slinging bales and lifting calves once he learned to walk. He was tremendous, though he wore the muscle lean over a long frame of greater than six feet such that he appeared more equine than bear-like. The ball made such a terrific sound off his bat when he struck it squarely that it would echo off the wood of the grandstand and the wall and resound off the iron of the bridge adjacent. He once cracked a pitcher's shinbone with a sharp drive, bending the lower portion of the man's leg complete in the wrong direction as though it were hinged. It flapped impotently as the man thrashed and wailed while they carried him off and laid him in a cart to be pulled to a doctor who, it turned out, set the leg improperly such that the pitcher, the Silver Stars' best that year, thereafter walked unevenly on legs of disproportionate length. He eventually returned to play but could no longer run, which limited his effectiveness.

With Stroud and Tiny dancing impatiently off third and second respectively, Davis, who'd been fooled into swinging through the dipper on the first pitch, got a flat one of only average speed and met the ball true. The report was among the sharpest and loudest he'd ever produced. It split the first and second basemen and rose no higher than twelve feet off the ground on its way to striking the fence in right, wherefrom issued a spray of splinters and debris. The impact caused a notch that Robinson would repair the next day with an unpainted board, which remained conspicuous until the following week when the groundskeeper was able to secure a new can of green paint.

Both Stroud and Tiny Kincardine, who earned his nickname by measuring a quarter inch shorter than his brother, scored easily. Davis had his eye on a three-base hit but when he neared third the right fielder's throw, relayed by the first baseman, got away from the third baseman on an awkward bounce. Though Davis had dropped into an explosive slide he popped up on contact with the bag in a cloud of dust and allowed his momentum to carry him over, then regained his feet and dashed for home. The base minder had turned to scamper after the ball, which he found and sent on to the catcher, who was standing astride the dish, waiting.

Davis barrelled toward his objective with a terrifying velocity and the amassed determination of a man who'd felt since his adolescence that he'd something to prove to the world. The catcher stood, the ball clutched at his midsection, now his navel, now at his chest as he prepared for an impact. It is unclear if the Redstarts' catcher was an especially religious man, but several who witnessed what came next—three men in the front row immediately behind the site of the event, and Carney the umpire— would later affirm that they heard him uttering a prayer as Davis neared. Davis would say that he heard nothing but saw quite clearly the terror in the man's eyes, for while it would be considered routine for a man so employed to endure collisions while defending the dish, there could be few collisions of such force. Davis with a full head of steam was formidable as the Jupiter or any 4-4-0 locomotive you care to name, and just as likely to harm anyone foolish enough to stand in his way.

Carney moved toward the rear and a little up the line, both in order to see the play more cleanly and because he sensed that there might be objects sent airborne in the wake of the pileup and he feared for his safety. Women were seen to cover their eyes.

Davis lowered his right shoulder because he wanted to protect his throwing arm, and it was that part of his body, mounded and rock solid, that first met the catcher, driving up under his chin and sending aloft the wire mask that he'd neglected to shed. The man's face seemed to ride Davis's shoulder for a time as the red-stockinged backstop left his feet and flew backwards. Davis attested to the belief that at this point the man had already lost consciousness, which certain other observers would maintain could be the only explanation for the manner in which the smaller party had gone so limp, tossed ragged like crêpe in a gale. The most diminutive whinny issued from the catcher's lips, full of surprise and pathos, or possibly simply the sound of whole lungsful of air being forced too quickly through the windpipe.

Heavens, said Henslow.

A pinkish trail of blood diluted by snot arced through the air over Davis's shoulder as the prone man's head flopped backward, a line of viscous stuff landing as a squiggle in the dust quite near where the ball came to rest after being dislodged from the catcher's grasp. The pair of players separated slightly in midair, the unconscious party falling sack-like while Davis tensed his limbs in preparation for the landing. He came down on the catcher's head with his knee and shin, and in the outrun of his crash he rolled off the man's body as his foot made contact with the plate. Carney made the safe call, then motioned toward the Redstarts' bench for some men to come to the assistance of their fallen mate. They carried him off and laid him behind the visitors' bench where they worked to revive him with salts and cold water.

It happened that the blow to the head, in addition to the loss of consciousness, had ruptured a sinus cavity, which in due time developed infection, which in turn began to affect this man's vision. He experienced a blurring and several spots of darkness in his sight, and so was not able to catch a ballgame again.

The Redstarts evinced no ill will toward Davis—it was a rotten trick of timing and nothing more. Certainly they themselves had delivered such knockouts to opposing players. Davis was allowed to continue in the game because no infraction of the rules had occurred.

With the three runs across and a bencher suiting up and jogging in to take the injured man's place, the Londoners buckled down and retired the next three Pine Groves— Poppel, Tip, and Lehmann—on cleanly fielded ground balls. The sides traded twos in the fourth inning, and the Redstarts added a single in the fifth. McCurdle led off the seventh with a two-base hit, and after Davis struck out, Tip laced a triple that rattled off the wall in left, scoring McCurdle, and then Poppel knocked Tip in. In the eighth, tiring, Poppel then gave up five consecutive hits which allowed London three tallies to bring it to 7–6 Ashburnham, but then corrected himself with encouragement from the stomping, whistling crowd.

In the ninth he induced two groundouts to Tiny before the Redstarts' third baseman came up. Poppel heaved a slow-churning looper that the third baseman ripped right back at the box, where Poppel stood with his arm still outstretched toward the hitter. The ball flew straight at his hand and smashed into it directly with terrific force. The tip of his index finger split open, the nail cleaved right down its middle forming a kind of gully there, angry and ragged and pouring forth blood. The ball ricocheted to Davis but he had no play so the runner stood safe at first.

Henslow stalked out to meet Poppel and marvel at the river of blood. Goodness, boy, he said, can you continue? I can bring McCurdle in.

No, it's just one more man. I can get him. He wiped the digit along the thigh of his trousers, but the blood kept coming.

Carney took a few strides out from behind the plate. Are you able to go on? he asked.

Yes, sir, yes, I'm fine, said Poppel, and retook his position. When he threw the blood spun off the ball as it sailed homeward, but he gutted through and pitched two strikes before the batter popped out to Tiny at third. Then the Pine Groves converged on the mound to pat one another on the back and to ask Poppel how he fared.

Does it hurt? asked Stroud.

Mother's cunt, it hurts, Poppel answered.

Then you'll need a drink, said Black.

Theirs was an age notable for the ease with which a man might disappear in order to escape judgment or responsibility. This was especially true there, in southern Ontario, with its proximity to an international border, rail lines and waterways carrying figures and cargo to desolate Superior in the west, and in the east to the Atlantic Ocean, and everything beyond. But it was the case everywhere that surety rested on flimsy testimonials and handwritten documents, and so much of the map remained unimaginably remote. It was consequently reasonable to assume that some of the people you knew were not who you knew them to be. They were criminals, deadbeats, welshers, or escapees.

McCurdle was none of these and was in fact McCurdle—and everything in this account about him is verifiably true—but about the others we might be less sure. Klopp, for one, who was not Klopp as McCurdle well knew but a serial bigamist of a different name who'd been run out of Montreal for having three wives, all of them under the age of fifteen, and two of them with child when he'd fled. This McCurdle knew because Klopp had become talkative one evening at Potter's over several glasses of uncut whisky. It was a confidence loosely offered but which McCurdle would keep. It explained the catcher's habits, certainly, and McCurdle thought it better that Long Tom move among street women in fair exchanges of currency and service, with fewer lies in the negotiation than had doubtless featured in his former life. Where he'd acquired his current wife McCurdle was not quite certain, but he was assured that she was a good deal older than fifteen. Whoever Klopp had once been he caught a good game and that was worth a great deal to McCurdle.

It was generally accepted that Feeney, as another example, had been a priest in the northwest but was defrocked for reasons unknown or kept in confidence among the ballplaying fraternity. Whatever his past crimes he was held in such esteem by the boys, his eye the object of such devoted faith, that they called him Old Judge as often as they did his surname.

This mutability was also the cause for the presence of so many ghost entries in the box scores of the day. Players would assume and discard identities in response to the events of their lives, the financial pressures and threats; they drifted into towns and latched on, slipping out again just as suddenly. Officialdom asserted that most of said entries reflected only botched transcriptions or misheard names on the part of scorers or newspapermen, but that didn't square with lived reality, where the only constant from summer to summer seemed to be the baseline of corruption, grift, syndicalism, itinerance, and misrepresentation. These varieties of malfeasance certainly existed in all walks of life but appeared to be concentrated around the game. It was a slick business that attracted slick dealers.

According to McCurdle's considerable experience however, his current situation was relatively honourable, the South Western less ridden with corruption than most leagues. He'd played in circuits wherein your success was a direct reflection of the gamblers' confidence in your team's abilities: if they liked you, your side was likely to attract more capital that might be redirected into the umpire's pocket, thereby all but assuring victory. That didn't seem to be the case in the South Western. Not unless McCurdle's sensitivity to his surroundings had begun to fail him.

The Biltmores remained the cream of the league heading into the last weekend of June, and if the Pine Groves didn't make ground fast the Guelph-based club would take the first-half crown, ensuring their place in the championship series at season's end. The first half was set to end with a break to recognize Dominion Day followed by second-half games commencing July 7. The second-half winner would face the first half's best over the first and, if necessary, second weekends in September. If the same side took both the first and second halves the championship series would be waived. In years past upon such an occurrence a match pitting All-Star teams against one another was organized for the victors' grounds, with the gate as compensation for their troubles and recognition of their glory.

It was tempting to assign prescience to the compilers of the season's schedule, to believe in the possibility of a grand design, but surely those responsible could not have known with certainty that the Biltmores would be out front in late June with the Pine Groves in close pursuit. Nevertheless, there it was in black ink on newsprint: the Ashburnhams boarded the Grand Trunk on the morning of June 23, bound for Guelph via Toronto, with the first-half title in the balance. Lose but one of the four scheduled matches and the Groves would be runners-up.

Carriages conveyed them to the park, a trim, well-kept diamond in a lush and leafy corner of the local Exhibition Grounds. A single covered bank of grandstand seating rose behind home plate, with benches and room for picnicking along the baselines, and no outfield fence, simply more grass running on toward a row of stately elms, the closest roughly five hundred feet from the batter. This rectangular green was bounded on all sides by handsome residences of two and three storeys with cupolas and gables with contrasting trim.

It was terrifically humid at mid-afternoon and the air held a sheen of haze lending the distant elms the appearance of painting, a lush unreality which made their greens deeper and fuller and cast over all an aspect of Gethsemane. The scene prompted Henslow, wilting in his heavy suit, to intone, His sweat was as it were great drops of blood falling down to the ground.

No need to warm up at least, said Strom Keenan.

Not for a Christing bencher, said Lehmann, and Keenan said nothing more.

Clean up your fucking language, man, said Henslow.

Guelph pitched a rookie in that godawful heat, a town boy of papery complexion who had fair speed but poor accuracy. This angered the Pine Groves for though they knocked many hits against the boy it suggested the Biltmores felt assured they'd finish off Ashburnham sooner or later and needn't bother themselves too terribly over how it happened. A final of twelve to six in the Pine Groves' favour did nothing to quell their animosity. McCurdle pitched well enough though it was clear to most of the boys that he was taking something off, being judicious in the application of mustard because he knew he had to save some for Friday, and one or two tries on Saturday.

It happened that someone or other had come into possession of a case of Seagram's rye and so the Pine Groves enjoyed a lubricated night in at their hotel. Later it would come to be known that the liquor was the gift of a local Biltmore supporter of some means who'd reasoned that if you offer a ballplayer some whisky, he'll react like a dog to food and prove unable to stop himself. This was bound to negatively impact the Ashburnhams' play on Friday, and possibly it did, though not enough. Another steaming afternoon kept the muscles of McCurdle's arm unknotted and loose and he produced a gem, striking out each member of the host side at least once and two of them twice. They managed only weak dribblers. This McCurdle attributed to experimentation, a new grip that he felt might allow his ball to emulate the boggling trajectory shown by the London hurler's trick pitch. He got a deep diving motion on a ball that bit about three-fifths of the way to the plate leaving the batter little time to adjust his swing.

Davis and Lehmann hit the cover off the ball to back him, and the Pine Groves were a swept doubleheader away from sneaking up on the Biltmores from behind to claim the first-half laurels.

That night McCurdle noticed a new irritation located within the knob of his elbow, and this—alongside the routine pain higher up, and the burning and gnawing feeling in his smaller fingers—he was unable to quiet with what remained of his bottle of Seagram's. He was haunted too by an inability to precisely recall the finer details of Maureen's face, as well as her scent.

The Biltmores had a giant at first base whose trunk-like arms allowed him to swing a fearsome bat of unlikely proportion. He was called Haggerty, though McCurdle thought maybe he recognized him as a certain Gray, encountered years previous in the Empire League. But Haggerty, whoever he'd been at birth, was the Biltmores' star and Guelph's favoured adopted son, slashing and hacking his way through league batting records and propelling the side to great success. Five years after these events Haggerty would fall beneath a draught horse, and though he would hold on for four days he'd eventually succumb to his injuries. The people of Guelph would be so overcome with grief that the city's leaders would arrange to have a platform built on the back of a radial railway streetcar to parade Haggerty's casket around town, a local funeral train for a summertime diamond hero who'd brought esteem and thrills to the local spectating public.

Saturday's doubleheader began auspiciously but quickly became an ordeal for the Pine Groves. They went down quietly in the first, and then two men reached for Haggerty, whose forearms pulsed and swelled as he wagged his bat before stepping into the hitter's box. McCurdle's arm felt leaden. The crowd was disquieted and unruly in the unmoving heat. A bottle was thrown to the foot of the Ashburnham bench; jeers and insults peppered the air. It must have occurred to them that the unlikely scenario of the Pine Groves overtaking the Biltmores to claim the first-half title was now within the realm of possibility.

The left-handed Haggerty dug in and leered at McCurdle, who reared and fired his first pitch. Haggerty exploded into a smooth and mighty swing and clobbered it. It hit the trunk of the elm in dead centre after two bounces and then rebounded awkwardly, sending Cook scrambling. He reached the ball eventually—it was now lying inert in the grass of right centre—but his discombobulation pulled his throw offline, and Josephus Davis had to lope over to field it. By the time he was able to cock and fire there was no play to be made as Haggerty was already crossing the plate.

Haggerty's next trip to bat had a similar result, and by the seventh inning McCurdle was in significant pain and quite certain he wouldn't be able to lift his arm come Sunday morning. The score stood at 14–3 for the Biltmores and the crowd in the swelter was well in its cups. Vendors in white hats and coats hawked bags of salted peanuts from shoulder-slung baskets which made the patrons only crave drink more. They filed in a steady stream from the stands to the tavern adjacent which made brisk business offering beer and whisky shots in a serial fashion, a receiving line of liquid buttressing, the Biltmore boosters returning looser and more argumentative with each passing inning, smoking, chewing, cursing, and angling for altercation.

When McCurdle took his turn at bat in the seventh, he grimaced and said Ooaaah while taking his warmup swings. The cranks in the nearest seats got on him, saying, Oh, does it hurt to lose so badly, mick? Are you sore and tired? Whyn't you have a lie-down, you fuckin mick? Go on. McCurdle said nothing. After Tiny reached first on a poke over the shortstop's head, he strode to the plate with his lumber while Davis began to stretch and swing on deck. He's done, some of the hecklers continued, meaning McCurdle. Get him out, he needs a bed, the old man needs his rest.

You ought to stop your mouths, Davis said.

That's not precisely where all the trouble began, but it was likely the last point at which what came next could have been stopped. Things thereafter assumed a certain momentum that made reversal or cessation quite impossible.

You ought to fuck right back to whatever backwater you're from, said another spectator, which was enough for Davis, who strode over to the front of the grandstand and asked the man to repeat himself. Are you having difficulty understanding, you degenerate moron? the man said.

Davis pointed the bat head at the man while leaning over into the first row. Enough from you, he said. I'll have to come and quiet you down if you don't do it yourself.

Davis's use of the bat in this gesture apparently proved too provocative for several of the men present. Already the women in attendance were being ushered toward the back rows or out of the grandstand entirely and men were rolling up their sleeves. A bottle clipped Josephus's shoulder, then a partially full bag of cherries caught him on the chin. Hold on now, he said, and then everything broke open.

A man sitting near Davis stood suddenly and caught the slugger with a surprise haymaker to the ear. Davis recoiled and then raised his bat in a threatening manner, but was set upon by several others, the bat wrestled from his hands and lost somewhere in the mass.

McCurdle saw all this unfold from the batter's box and stepped out. The umpire turned and shouted, Easy, please. Calm, calm, or I'll have to call time. Then McCurdle stormed over and the adjudicator waved his hands, shouting, Time is called, time is called.

Alerted to the fracas, the remaining Pine Groves erupted from the bench, as did the Biltmores, and all congregated around Davis, who'd climbed over the partition and was standing among the seats with his fists raised trying to determine who'd decked him. Something else—a fist or a bottle or an elbow—caught him in the back of the head and, checking first to be certain no women remained in the vicinity, Davis began swinging wildly. The other players spilled over the short wooden wall and were now among the spectators too, battling one another as well as civilians with utter heedlessness for who they might be assaulting.

Everywhere men appeared grateful for the opportunity to indulge their brutal natures. Bowlers and straw boaters went airborne and came down to litter the ground. There being so many would-be Plug Uglies present, bricks were employed, and bats taken up, swung indiscriminately to meet necks, backs, skulls, and forearms raised in defense.

With three thousand spectators and two dozen ballplayers present there proved no shortage of participants, and the melee spread to include many of them though no precise count was performed. An account published in a newspaper originating from Kitchener claimed that a reporter attending had witnessed approximately eighty bloodthirsty souls engaged in fisticuffs, though it would emerge that this was based on simple hearsay. McCurdle would've guessed fewer than that were seriously interested and actually throwing punches, while Henslow, observing from the distance of the pitcher's box, would claim with certainty that two hundred were actively implicated.

Whatever the numbers, it was attested that the Pine Groves were not overmatched, delivering as well as they received. Tiny and Tip stood back-to-back, swinging wildly, and Tip at least clocked one gentleman so soundly in the jaw that he crumpled instantly. Long Tom stood several rows up the grandstand, spread his arms, and launched himself onto the pile, bringing down many in street clothes and a few Biltmores besides, landing eventually with his knee upon the temple of Arterton, the Guelph catcher.

For the home side, the imposing Haggerty settled on a strategy of separating individuals from the heart of things, pulling men off the pile one at a time, walking them back toward home plate, bashing them once or twice about the face, and then going back in to extract another. He did Black, Cook, and Keenan this way while Stroud managed to wriggle free and return to the seething heap to land more blows on several heads. Haggerty fixed his eyes on McCurdle, who was occupied in grappling with an off-duty constable, and made for him but was intercepted by Lehmann who leapt like a puma from a tree limb and surprised Haggerty. The two rolled across the turf where, once righted, Haggerty drove his knee into Lehmann's groin, causing Bon's vision to become spotted, but he regained his senses and headbutted Guelph's big hitter, breaking the bridge of his nose and bringing forth a great torrent of blood which the injured party simply wiped with his sleeve and spit away, saying, That won't be enough. He then locked his left arm around Lehmann's neck, bent him over at the waist and squeezed while landing a series of quick knocks into his face, the net effect of which was to silence Bon, who sank to the grass, slack as a rag.

Someone twisted McCurdle's arm behind his back and wrenched so intently that it was as if they'd known his weakness. McCurdle spat invectives, then twisted out of the hold and jabbed so swiftly into the first face he saw upon wheeling around that the gent crossed his eyes and sank slowly to his knees, a light dimming and then snuffed.

As the fighters tired they became sloppier and more careless, and pugilism gradually gave way to tussles and aggrieved embraces. Words were tossed like cudgels. Everywhere men were bloodied and dazed. And while the violence was terrifying it can't be denied that the combatants all experienced a kind of ecstasy in their limbs, in the cheeks and guts and kidneys receiving blows, in their arms and fists and feet delivering them. Klopp found McCurdle's eyes at one early point in the proceedings and grinned to say isn't this a fine way to spend a Saturday afternoon.

In the end a contingent of police in uniform arrived to break things up and once audible again, the umpire—who'd spent much of the battle standing next to Henslow, narrating the action and occasionally tsk-tsking the disputants, as though order had never been his to maintain—called the game, and the second leg of the doubleheader to boot. The police established a cordon like a tourniquet, removing the bad element from the greater mass of people. They moved in with truncheons swinging, aiming for knees, shins, heads, seeming as dark hearted as the brawlers, but very shortly the character of the bloody gathering seemed to shift in recognition of the conflict's flimsy pretext.

Once separated the skirmishers stood upright where possible, brushed themselves off, and looked to be reunited with their hats. Men who only a moment previous had pledged to murder one another unearthed within themselves a cautious civility which saw them collaborate to put right the items and objects they'd upended. Several handshakes were exchanged, and congratulations offered for successes in the affray. Mighty good uppercut, lad. Boy, I thought your chokehold would end me. I haven't been hit that hard since father's last drink.

As this curious postbellum scene unfolded the men checked themselves and one another for damage. Klopp had received two black eyes, while Poppel had his lower lip torn by a mean clawing. Black's left earlobe was bitten right through and would require a stitch. Keenan had taken several good kicks and was sore the length of the left side of his torso; the pain in his ribs suggested that one or more of them were broken and over the ensuing days the skin would turn blue and then black.

With the day's competition cancelled, and many hours before their return trip to Ashburnham via Toronto, the Pine Groves were rounded up and loaded into carriages. They were guided to a secluded place not far away, near the confluence of two rivers where the water rushed fast but shallow, so that the men could wade in to bathe and to soothe their bruises and abrasions.

They removed and folded their uniforms to lay them upon dry rocks before jumping in. The water found them joyful in their bodies, the ease and release connecting them viscerally to moments of heightened sensation they'd long ago lived and still held precious.

Chas Hewitt, the bench player, recalled with elation an afternoon he and his wife had spent when they were young on the verandah-installed daybed of an uncle's farmhouse in Quebec, the smell of an imminent weather change, watching the afternoon light age in the valley below while distant highbacked cloudbanks dropped columns of rain on forested hillsides beyond.

Tip, who'd passed three years aboard a Moroccan-registered schooner barge, sank back into the memory of standing up to his chin in the bath-warm Tyrrhenian Sea off Naples under spangling starshine while receiving a gentle submarine fondling from a handsome mute deckhand they'd taken on in Malta.

Black was a son of the prairie who in a previous life had been a stoker and so revisited a moment aboard an unburdened engine flying across the flat pan of Saskatchewan, racing a stormfront that burped electricity and menace, the locomotive surging and the wind kicking up, the land in its stark Cartesian simplicity so parched and open that he could smell its yearning.

And for McCurdle, his dream of Maureen, and the open window through which he could only just see the soft velvety darkness above the blackness of the silhouetted trees. He had learned that in the days after seeing her he would find himself hollowed out for want, lost in the lea of her, and he felt himself tilting toward that same feeling there, among his teammates splashing and washing in the river. The sting of new wounds, the dull subdermal ache of fists landed, the agony searing his right arm familiar but heightened, his languid member wiggling in the warm current's quick. The heat had not relented but was growing less direct, radiating off the earth and the stones instead of beaming from above. At the water's edge shaggy old willows heaved and held, frisking the surface with their longest fronds. McCurdle lay back to fill his ears with the river's babble but the thoughts of her would not abate.

The teams' owners would meet two days later at Lamb's Inn near Cambridge, which was a neutral site chosen as the venue to settle the issue of the first-half standings. From that assembly they emerged to name the Biltmores the rightful winners, as well as to censure and fine Grafton on behalf of his players, it being determined that Davis and McCurdle had been the wrongful actors in the event. Grafton protested and maintained his players' victimhood and threatened convincingly to pull his team from the association, but after much debate the financial penalty was greatly reduced and the brewer recognized that the exposure granted his Pine Grove brand ale by having the team in the loop resulted in sales far greater than any such amercement could offset. He resolved only that his side would come roaring into the season's second half with a score to settle, and woe be upon all scheduled opponents, including and especially the Biltmores.

There followed strange nights of murderous heat and vexing liminality. It was difficult to identify the edges of things. Forests to the north and west had erupted into flame and plumes of smoke drifted over Ashburnham, producing an orange pall and a choking dryness and very little wind stirred to move the air through. The sun appeared lost and forlorn, a dim speck in the prevalent murk. Birds quelled their songs and the wolves that roamed in packs to the north of the town made odd calls of a sort not heard before nor since.

On the night of July 10, McCurdle's thirty-seventh birthday—or at least the thirty-seventh anniversary of the date recorded on his birth record (of the birth year being 1855, all in a position to hold the knowledge felt secure)—the full moon shone devilishly red like a single diseased eye peering through the darkness to observe his pitiable state. He and the other Pine Groves had sweltered through a twelve-day layoff as the first-half results were allowed to settle and the teams prepared themselves for the back end of the schedule. They were for those nearly two weeks labourers only, baseball a distant memory that came to them when they nursed their many injuries collected both via the campaign's natural stresses and the calamity at Guelph.

From that latter event, it arose that Keenan's ailments were worse than originally surmised. Two ribs had indeed been broken, but also as it happened a hernia had dilated through the cavity formed by the breakage, which in turn had become wracked with infection such that the poor man had taken to his bed and not moved from it in ten days. Where originally the question posed had been when the versatile bench player might return to the team, it had become, as the days mounted, whether or not he would ever play again.

When games recommenced the Poets of Stratford paid a visit to the Quaker Grounds on the banks of the Whetung. McCurdle, feeling less a shearing pain in his arm and more a low humming ache, battled through a back-and-forth match, giving up six runs but helping with a timely double to eke out a 7–6 win. On Friday Davis made easy work of the Poets with three doubles and a base on balls, and McCurdle threw well enough to strand many Stratfordians on base, making for two quick wins in a row for the Pine

Groves. Saturday a much-needed rain fell and no base-ball was in the offing.

By the following Thursday, when the Silver Stars trained into town, it was common knowledge that Keenan's condition was grave, and so Saturday's games were announced as benefits to ease his misfortune. Henslow spoke through a bullhorn and sung Keenan's praises as the most loyal and adaptable Pine Grove while the players walked the seating rows with their hats turned up accepting coins and bills, as well as a note from Peavey the grocer offering a month's free orders to the wounded man.

McCurdle climbed the grandstand with his cap in his left hand, his right too weak after having pitched two more games, Thursday and Friday, splitting them. He could scarce lift the afflicted limb above his belt.

Detecting this during earlier pregame activities, Klopp spoke with him in confidence as they both stood near the bench. What are you going to do then? Pitch with your left?

I applied some liniment that'll soak in, and I'll warm it up thoroughly.

Was it magic liniment?

It was not, you dogfucker.

More's the shame. I'll be praying for you, Mickey.

I could use it.

I pray you learn to pitch with your left.

After raising seventy-five dollars for Keenan, the boys went out and whipped the Silver Stars despite McCurdle's discomfort, the Kitchener side mustering very few good swings in either game. In the second the Pine Groves cruised so easily—holding a 9–0 lead in the fifth inning—that Henslow, at Klopp's suggestion, gave McCurdle the rest of the afternoon off.

Stroud's barber had indicated that the visitors had enjoyed a raucous evening the night before and that their state come the first pitch of the doubleheader would be less than optimal. It later came to light that Grafton himself had communicated to Potter that the out-of-towners should be offered a drastically reduced price on their ale, with the loss to be covered by Grafton. The owner had extended this manner of hospitality before—at great personal expense it should be noted, as ballplayers fairly earned their reputation as drinkers—and it generally did the trick. His willingness to do it again suggested the desperation with which he intended to pursue his goal of taking the second-half title and smashing the Biltmores in the culminating series.

Twin victories notwithstanding, a note of concern was sounded in the later innings of the first game when the manager had insisted on walking the Stars' ninth hitter with no runners aboard and none out. He very clearly relayed the sign for this to Klopp, who doubted he'd seen right and signalled to McCurdle to throw his fast one for a strike, which McCurdle did. Henslow called out after the umpire indicated the strike, Klopp, goddamnit, look at me. To hell with your damned insubordination—put him on! Walk him! Thoroughly confused, Klopp resolved to do as he'd been commanded and to later inquire of the manager's thinking. He stood and called for four wide ones and McCurdle cursed and shook his head and then did as he'd been instructed, after which the batter discarded his lumber and trotted down to first.

Mercifully the inning ended with no further damage when McCurdle threw high to the next batter and got him to pop one up on the infield. He then coaxed a ground ball up the middle that Davis fielded cleanly and flipped to Tip, who stepped on second before leaping balletically over the runner to throw on to first for the double retirement.

Once back at the bench Klopp calmly asked of Henslow why he'd felt it necessary to put the first man on, and through a set of names and described scenarios it became apparent that the circumstances which convinced the manager to attempt the strategy were either imagined or more likely remembered from a previous decade, perhaps an afternoon from his time with the National Association club from Troy, New York, for which he'd very briefly played.

What does any of that have to do with this here today, Cap? said Klopp.

The grey-eyed general looked out over the scene before them and a change came across his face, the lifting of a veil. Nothing at all, he said. Why are you talking nonsense, Klopp? Let's win this blasted ballgame, boys. Someone remind me of the score.

Someone did.

Of course, of course, said the weathered tactician.

Several of the players convened at Potter's after the second of the day's two victories had been entered in the log. As they downed their drinks, Lehmann said, By Christ we ought to do something before we find ourselves in a tight game and our manager is clucking like a goddamned chicken.

It's only age, said McCurdle. He's slipping a little. That can't be helped.

Henslow had always been a rock. The planets and stars in their prescribed revolutions could not have been more dependable than had been their dear old manager.

It's a disease he's got, said Lehmann. I ought to know— my own father went that way. Starts slow, then picks up, and before long it's awful.

Stroud asked, You think it'll go that way for old Henslow?

Always goes like that, said Lehmann, and then drank.

How long would you say? said McCurdle, opting not to mention anything of his experience with his own mother, whose loss bedevilled him each day and worse come night.

Damned if I know, said Lehmann. A month. Ten years. What I know is this: it will be clear to those around him that the time to act has arrived. He'll be quite changed. Fouling himself, wandering.

McCurdle nodded. Doesn't he get any say?

He'll need help to see it and likely won't agree. But you have to understand what's best for him. Nobody would choose to live like that. Not if they knew they were that way.

How did it go for your father?

The end was an ordeal.

How do you mean about the end? said Black.

He had to be helped to it. It was—and here Lehmann paused to find the word, exhaled, folded his tongue into the recess of a molar—untidy. He set the word on the table, and it was up to each man present to decide for himself what was meant by it. The matter seemed settled for Lehmann, his posture making plain his unwillingness to elaborate.

Herman Rudolph Staley was, through a series of shrewd dealings, the holder of several very lucrative drug patents, most of which he had manufactured near his home in Brockville. However he was arguably known more widely as the owner and greatest promoter of the Vireos Base-Ball Club. It was commonly held that he felt more pride in the latter than in the former, though it was the proceeds of his patented medicines which supported the team and allowed for such a high calibre of ball to be hosted in a locality the size of Brockville.

Its location on the St. Lawrence River granted the town easy access to the US market, and being situated at the intersection of the old Grand Trunk and Brockville & Ottawa lines, both of which were later to come under the CPR banner, further contributed to its advantageous position. In addition to playing ball McCurdle and his mates loaded and unloaded freight cars, stocking and shipping out of the Staley warehouse adjacent to downtown. The team was named in a winking fashion after a popular virility pill which shared with the players' stockings a lovely, soft shade of brown. They competed in the Ottawa and St. Lawrence League against company teams from across the wedge-shaped slice of map bordered to the north and south by those rivers, from Kingston and Arnprior at the westernmost to Cornwall in the east. The level of competition was several notches below that of the South Western Association, though as McCurdle was a few years away from playing in the latter he had as yet no direct way of knowing that. He was, though, far and away the best all-around player in the O&SL and enjoyed relative renown as a result, which might have been why he enjoyed so thoroughly his three years there.

Very shortly after their meeting McCurdle and Maureen took to convening on Sundays and one or two evenings during the week to stroll the riverside and watch the steamboats plying the water, and to sit on a bench beneath a particular oak to converse and simmer, their attraction to one another veritably narcotic in its intensity. When their thighs brushed obliquely McCurdle felt himself flush, his vision growing distant and all sounds in his ears taking on a muffled quality as though they'd been dropped into a large bottle.

The river sparkled so brilliantly in their eyes on one such Sunday in August that Maureen pulled the brim of her hat down and McCurdle cocked his boater to shade his face.

How many more games are there to play? she asked him coyly, as it was her belief even in those early days of their courtship that he would deliver a proposal at the conclusion of the season—his final season, she then assumed.

Three weeks, he said. About a dozen games.

Do you travel?

Only to Gananoque. Next week. The rest are here.

He squinted and risked a look up into her face, which was half lit and half in the shadow of her wide hat. He took in her right eye, which, as with the other, was a deep and luminous brown, the iris appearing almost too large for the space allotted it. She was already examining him, an appraisal or a request for a truth below the words they were both speaking, and a charge ran through his nervous system. Her eyebrows were thick and dark and there was the finest down on her cheek. In her high-necked cotton dress he could see only the shape of her shoulders and no skin but for her forearms and wrists, which were delicate but not thin. He wondered if the soft palpating skin where her veins were just visible was scented and fought the desire to raise her hand to his face.

Three weeks. And then you're done for the season. Her eye was fixed on him and did not waver.

Yes. We'll have secured the championship. We're well out ahead of Cornwall.

And when it's done, what will you do with all your time?

There may yet be some games. Staley likes to parade us about. He schedules exhibitions.

But it will be quieter, surely.

It's fair to say that. So I'll continue to work. And to see you, I'd like to think.

That's your wish?

My very fervent wish, yes.

That coincides with mine, so that's fine.

Very fine.

Indeed upon the season's conclusion the Vireos were champions and after two additional weekend exhibitions Mc-Curdle's time was his own. In fact it was Maureen who quite brazenly proposed they steam up to Ottawa where the leaves were in their first blush and take two rooms at a fine hotel and dine in nice establishments before returning on Sunday. McCurdle agreed before she'd completed her proposal.

After dinner which included wine they strolled in the evening lamplight, she hooking her arm in his. Once back at the Russell House hotel they took seats at the long bar and enjoyed brandies and McCurdle smoked a good cigar. He touched her hands. She risked a peck on his cheek, and later when he knocked on her door she answered in a robe and took him into her bed, where he remained until dawn.

That remained their sole carnal assignation, though their charged entanglement continued as the weather cooled and the tourist boats thinned on the St. Lawrence and then stopped frequenting the river. On a Tuesday afternoon in late October news came that Staley, who had been visiting business interests in Boston, had been involved in a collision between carriages and was gravely injured. The shocking information raced through Brockville like a contagion. It reached McCurdle and Maureen who were sitting together at Mrs. Morgan's Tea House and there opened beneath them both something like a deep black pit, an area of uncertainty where earlier there had been only solid ground, dimly lit perhaps but dependable in its location.

Staley was dead within a week. All of Brockville was draped in black, and all business ceased for three days. His young widow was counselled that it would be wiser to profit immediately than to attempt to learn her late husband's business on the fly and assume control of the company, which was after all large and complex, thereby risking failure. The patents were sold one by one at great prices, and with these funds Mrs. Staley and her three small children relocated to New York City. By Christmas all operations in Brockville were shuttered, and the Vireos disbanded, their roster raided for its strongest players, the rest scattered to disparate circuits or back to lives as fieldhands, in lumber camps, or as charity mission tramps. McCurdle jumped to the Empire then, and so began his itinerance, leaving Maureen in Brockville to wait for him to settle into a life with her.

At Christmas next he returned to Brockville for two days, tired and downhearted at the thought of a second year spent in the sandstone quarry at Potsdam but there being no reasonably equivalent ballclub nearer Maureen.

They had not been together since he'd left Brockville in February to make his way in the Empire league, and his impression was that she'd grown in confidence. He'd detected this in her letters but had not yet seen it in her personally. She carried herself worldly and wise and spent her leisure time reading novels and magazines, memorizing poetry. She read sonnets aloud to her students.

Do you think about me when I'm away? said McCurdle in the parlour of her boarding house.

Haply I think on thee, she said, and then my state, like to the lark at break of day arising from sullen earth, sings hymns at heaven's gate.

Do you think of me in a sinnerly manner, though?

This she answered not in words but with a kiss followed by a smile.

You know I'm still interested in being your husband. If you're still warm to the idea.

I will marry you, McCurdle, she said, once you're fixed in place. I won't marry an itinerant.

The soft scolding elicited a strange thrill in him. I'll be secure, he said.

He was sincere, for he sought to undertake the creation of a lineage that denied where he came from in order to privilege the person he'd made himself become. What was more he wanted the child or children to be not his but theirs. Hers and his. He wanted to name a boy Ransom Chatwin McCurdle after meeting a hotelier named Ransom in Syracuse. He thought it a fine name.

See that you are, she said and gave that smile once more.

After the Silver Stars left Ashburnham a damp settled over the river and environs, with rain falling almost consistently for eight days, washing out the next scheduled series against the Maroons. Consequently the players found themselves with extra time, much of which they spent taking turns sitting vigil with their stricken mate Keenan in his small rented room, its air sour and thick with miasmic emanations. On Friday evening as the rain fell outside the small window McCurdle took his turn. He and Keenan had not been especially close, though McCurdle had never had any problem with the bencher in the season and a half they'd been rostered together. McCurdle understood the necessity of what he and the other players were doing as it seemed Keenan had no family nearby and there surely couldn't be anything quite as harrowing as facing your end alone.

Keenan's face was wan and waxy, his lips dry, hair plastered to his forehead. He'd tried to sit up, and while he fought and struggled to get into a comfortable position, McCurdle saw that the bandage wrapped around the sick man's abdomen was yellow and darkly splotched and ragged. Keenan saw him looking and explained that he no longer bothered to change it because it had dried in place and there would be such pain involved in removing it. He said, Now I guess it's just holding me together a while longer.

Come on now, McCurdle said, supposing that he should not be so upfront about Keenan's impending death but instead attempt to inspire him to rally. You'll get out of this. You'll be suiting up against the Biltmores and helping us stuff those pigfuckers. We need you, Keenan.

Oh, no, Mick. I'm done. And it's fine. I've got a nice spot waiting under a big elm tree. Very pretty. I'm not fearful of the ending. Yes, he said, the world is dark, and living is hard, and people can wound you. People and things. My father lost an arm to a fencepost while on horseback, and life was very hard for him after that. Sometimes when drinking he'd confide that it'd have been better if he'd lost his head and died right away. And that seems right.

It can be hard, agreed McCurdle.

Might not be so bad if it weren't for these mutinous bodies. Do you recall a day without pain? Keenan asked him.

Oh yes, said McCurdle, but not many. One or two. He thought not of ballgames but of the best days and the lone night with Maureen, and of taking pleasure in her and with her in the whole pulsing, aromatic world. Yes, just one or two.

I'd say my experience was the same, said Keenan. He closed his eyes and grimaced and then was quiet for a time.

McCurdle looked out the window where the rain had slowed and finding it quite still and hot in the room he lifted the sash to allow some fresh air to enter. He thought perhaps Keenan was sleeping or even that he had passed on until Keenan spoke up.

That's nice, he said feebly but clearly. It's good to get some clean air.

Yes, said McCurdle, breathe it in.

A lot of awfulness in this life, Keenan offered. But there was goodness, he said, there was light.

At about nine o'clock that evening Keenan did fall asleep and McCurdle stood and left and went out into the puddled street. No other player arrived to sit with the patient and it came that he died late in the night and was found in the morning by his landlady who'd entered the room to ask if Keenan was up to eating something for breakfast.

The players were quite affected. Henslow was especially upset, as he'd meant to visit the very morning that Keenan's death was discovered, and worried that if he'd only arrived earlier he might have been of some assistance, but some supposed it for the best he hadn't. The old man might have conflated Keenan's death with someone else's and so found himself in a sense adrift in time and weeping not for his bencher but for a long-dead loved one or relation.

For McCurdle it prompted him to revisit thoughts he'd had before concerning how an ordinary person could pass from the world of things and into the realm of memory, where they would reside in something like purgatory until all those who knew them died and then they simply ceased to be anything to anyone—like his mother would when he himself lost his life at some future date.

Keenan's elder brother was still living, a leathersmith in Toronto. He was sent for, and the following Wednesday made the journey as the Pine Groves and a full grandstand of three thousand mourners paid tribute to their fallen man in a persistent drizzle. The coffin rested on a pair of sawhorses over home plate, and a lectern stood just beyond, a few feet short of the pitcher's box, set there so that Grafton, Henslow, and Klopp could eulogize. The team donned black armbands which they would wear with their uniforms for the rest of the season. Keenan's body was then taken by train back to Toronto and laid as he'd said it would be in St. Michael's, though the following winter a visitor, among the most fervent of the Pine Grove boosters, went to pay his respects at the graveside and reported back that there was no elm tree overhead, or if there had been it had since fallen.

Warm and dry weather blew over the province thereafter, and the Ashburnhams minus poor Keenan spent much of Thursday in oven-hot train cars in transit to Kitchener in anticipation of two games Friday and two Saturday against the very same Silver Stars they'd lately faced in Ashburnham. The Stars were then occupying the lowest tier of the South Western, suffering from ineffective pitching and a porous defense. However the Pine Groves were not in their best fit for the first two games, played on a blazing hot afternoon at the Eby diamond before a decent crowd who sat sweating and fanning themselves and quaffing smuggled pilsners or spiked lemonades. The Silver Stars hung four on McCurdle in the first inning of the opener and added one per inning thereafter in a queer numerical trick that none on the Pine Groves' bench could recall having seen before. In the end McCurdle was responsible for all twelve Kitchener marks and none of the six that his side scratched out. Henslow, sensing the loss in the early going, asked McCurdle if he was in shape to continue to absorb the onslaught. The hurler responded in the affirmative, prompted by the same impulse toward self-obliteration which prompted him to imbibe until his eyes stopped seeing. Indeed any improvement he had felt in his arm as a result of the days-long layoff had already been erased in the early going, when he overthrew a zipper to the third batter and sensed something like a cord snapping somewhere between his elbow and his wrist. For the remainder of the game his arm was rubbery and alive with pain and felt at the shoulder as though the parts had been improperly fitted together. When seated on the bench awaiting his turn at the plate he couldn't use it to lift a water pail to his lips.

Henslow called in Hewitt for the capper and told McCurdle he'd go with Poppel for both of the Saturday tilts, and though the pain made it seem likely McCurdle would vomit if he gave himself the chance, he was stung by his manager's decision because there seemed to be no force nor circumstance capable of dulling his torrid ambition. Of course his only audible response was, Sure, Cap.

Hewitt started strong but his luck dried up in the sixth, and though Davis and Lehmann were both hitting the stuffing out of the ball none of the others seemed interested in or capable of generating much in the way of scoring, McCurdle included. He stood in centre letting the low late-day sun dry the sweat on his face and feeling the tight heat in his skin, angry with himself and thinking whether he should have taken the disbanding of the Vireos all those years back as his cue to leave ball diamonds and sore arms and train rides behind him and settle into a life with Maureen. It might after all be true that the howling ambition of the sort he possessed is a feral animal that is best killed early, held underwater until it no longer twitches.

After the two losses, McCurdle found his room overly hot even late into the evening and so sought the comfort of the hotel's club which was located in the basement where the stone walls radiated a delicious coolness.

It could easily be said that the Silver Star Hotel in Kitchener—which was owned by a Mr. Meier, who was also the principal shareholder in the ballclub—offered the finest accommodations on the whole South Western circuit. Unique among South Western Association teams the Silver Star players did not perform dirty unthinking labour but rather spent their working hours dressed finely and serving diners in the restaurant, or porting luggage as bellhops, or togged in white smocks and hats while cooking in the well-appointed kitchen. It was however known in certain circles that Meier also hired out some of his burliest employees and ballplayers to business owners across the region as strike-breakers to deal with unruly Nine Hour advocates. Select Stars were from time to time, when such need arose, enlisted to soften up knots of canal builders, miners, and railroad men, always while wearing black balaclava masks to conceal their identities and prevent as much as possible the acquisition of facial injury. Those who came back with black eyes or crooked noses were given a few days free of hotel work and also kept out of the lineup, as many of the ballplayers they faced were labour men and might recognize their assailants, and Meier was doubly concerned with maintaining the periodic infusion of revenue and keeping his ballclub afloat.

McCurdle found Stroud in the hotel's club enjoying a whisky and soda. He joined him at a small table, but after that drink Stroud professed exhaustion and retired to his room so McCurdle moved to the bar and ordered a beer.

You're with the Ashburnham club, aren't you? said the barman, a portly and grey-haired man with a friendliness in his eyes.

I am. McCurdle.

Ah, yes. Understand our boys undid you today.

We had a bad afternoon, yes. Many of us are still under a cloud from having just lost one of our ranks.

I heard. It made the paper here. My sympathies.

Thank you.

But surely by tomorrow you'll be back in form. The Stars are not on your level this year. It's hard for a company man to say, but it's plain as day and can't be denied.

They've been competitive in recent years.

We were better in my day.

You played.

Johnson. Third base, mostly.

I'm afraid I'm not familiar with your name, Mr. Johnson.

That's not surprising, Mr. McCurdle. I wasn't much of a ballplayer. The weakest member of that team, I'd admit. I could slap out a dribbler, steal a base. I was passable at third. But we had some real humdingers. Broonzy, Tettleton. Took the title in seventy-one, squeezed out the team from Galt. This was before the Stars moved up to the South Western, of course.

I've heard of Tettleton, I think.

Likely the same, yes. He jumped to the Maroons in seventy-three.

Of course.

Is what I'm hearing about your arm true?

Oh, hell. What in the Jesus are you hearing about my arm?

Some of the boys say it's gone dead. Nothing like how he'd thrown back in May, one told the other.

McCurdle took a long gulp of beer using his left hand. It's sore. Been a long season. Everybody's got their aches this time of the year. I'll be fine.

Oh, sure.

McCurdle began to suspect Johnson was specifically directed to glean these sorts of whisperings in aid of the home side. He put the glass down and looked into Johnson's red, watery eyes shining in the flickering lamplight and knew he had to decide whether to confront the spy or change the subject. He said, Do they keep all of you on with jobs?

A good many. None so long as me. Twenty years now since my last game for the Stars, and still I'm here. Mr. Meier's been good to me.

McCurdle tried to imagine life after base-ball. Maureen was there, he hoped, but he couldn't fill in the rest of the scene. What would he do for a living? Where would he live?

Johnson was reading his mind. Does your brewery keep you boys around after their playing days are behind them?

Sometimes, said McCurdle, though he couldn't come up with a single name.

Where's home, then?

I'm not exactly sure, said McCurdle, then finished his beer, put a coin on the bar top and excused himself.

In his room he stripped to his shorts, rubbed a pungent salve into the muscles of his shoulder and his triceps, then lay on a towel spread out on the floor near the open window and slept there fitfully until he woke sore all over in the morning.

Poppel cruised in both games on Saturday and McCurdle rallied to do damage with his legs, in one instance stealing second and third after taking a beanball to the kidney. He slid headfirst on his belly because already he could feel an angry contusion on his lower back that he didn't wish to exacerbate, but when he dove into third his right forearm jammed up against the defender's shoe and drove his humerus back up into the joint, stretching and twisting the ligaments and possibly tearing some for good. When Tip rapped one way out over the left fielder's head McCurdle was able to jog home while keeping the limb mostly immobilized until he sat, but within minutes there was tremendous swelling in the shoulder and it began to stiffen. He ducked into the clubhouse and attempted to wrap the joint tightly to keep the swelling at bay and perhaps maintain the use of it, but it did no good, and at the bottom of the inning it was Cook manning centre. McCurdle's day was done but for the long ride aboard a rattler all the way back to Ashburnham.

Having split four in Kitchener while the Biltmores ran the table against the Astonishers, the Pine Groves returned home beneath an inflated deficit and quite downtrodden in their mannerisms.

These were games the Groves should have won, opined Baxter Welt in black ink, as the Silver Stars are the bottom dwellers of the South West, deserving of a quartet of trouncings at Ashburnham's hands. It's nothing but a disgrace that

Henslow's men failed to complete their mission and with that failure find themselves at an even greater disadvantage to the Biltmores of Guelph. The season wanes, and our boys' chances slip further by the wayside with each defeat.

Christing lambfucker, muttered Henslow as he read the above while standing upon the Ashburnham platform waiting for his trunk to be delivered, his face owlish, his moustache damp and drooping.

McCurdle, overhearing this though he knew it was not meant for his ears, felt compelled to chime in. Baxter Welt's hackishness is an embarrassment to this town, he said. He knows nothing.

Looking up, Henslow said, He'd be forgettable if he didn't have Grafton's confidence. Spencer eats up everything he prints.

Fucking squirrelfucker.

Securely employed squirrelfucker, narrowed Henslow. Don't run onto the wrong side of him if you want to remain in Grafton's employ.

These, McCurdle would later reflect, were among the last cogent words his once esteemed manager would ever speak to him.

Where previously McCurdle's arm bothered him primarily when throwing but left him undisturbed when taking his swings at the plate, there arose in the aftermath of his rough slide a new hitch in the hitting motion, a click accompanied by a clenching that rendered the exercise noticeably less smooth than his regular stroke. The effect was that he could not swing freely, could not produce power at the level to which he was accustomed. He began to flail and to look lost on even the sweetest cookies, the slow pitches sitting fat and straight over the plate. Henslow, at Long Tom Klopp's whispered suggestion, moved McCurdle down in the order, first to fifth, and then to seventh, though to move him below that was still unthinkable. He was getting the odd infield slapper, beating out throws, and could place a bunt on the ace of hearts, but his average was in steep decline and the Pine Groves were in dire straits, the Biltmores pulling steadily away from them.

Henslow too continued to slip and now it was primarily McCurdle and Klopp managing the club in all practical terms. The two longest-tenured Pine Groves would arrive at the park early to make their suggestions as the faltering field boss pencilled in a shaky hand the names he'd all but forgotten, Klopp and McCurdle reminding him of their spellings, the players' handedness, the positions they regularly played. They would present in-game decisions as ideas thought aloud and appended, What do you think, Cap? And the aging general would assent decrepitly and it would be done.

It did not appear in print, but Baxter Welt declared in a manner meant to be overheard one evening at Potter's that Grafton's aim was to let the manager see things through to the end of the campaign before allowing him to bow out with dignity.

It was clear to the players, however, that if any dignity was to be salvaged a quicker intervention would be required. Though a rabid competitor, Henslow had long been remarked to have the strength to forgive a man his failings of eyesight or judgment, and it might be hoped that such forgiveness would be extended to him—a reserve of goodwill on which might be drawn the charity that would allow him to slip quietly from view with all the decency due him.

McCurdle was ill with it, devastated to watch a man who'd comported himself in a manner to inspire uniform respect among his charges and opponents alike come so unwound in so public a fashion. He was furious with an inattentive god who would deny such a man his rightful grace and furious with Grafton for prolonging the public ordeal. It was clear to anyone with an interest in the Pine Groves that their hardnosed, wise, and crafty Henslow was gone, replaced by a bumbling, forgetful, helpless fool. Unshaven, unkempt, in stained clothes, Henslow sat at the end of the bench appearing lost and frightened—that is, if he found his way to the field at all, there being several instances whereon he neglected to appear or was found on an Ashburnham streetcorner unable to tell whomsoever had intercepted him where he intended to be. On such days it was simply announced to all interested parties that the Pine Groves' leader had taken ill.

McCurdle had some trouble locating an interval when the company's owner was available and he himself was not on the company's time. On several occasions he would dash from the grainhouse floor to the administrative building adjacent hoping to catch Grafton still in his luxuriously furnished office, only to be told by staff there that Mr. Grafton had had business elsewhere. The dark part of McCurdle's mind found deceit in these statements and assumed that Grafton had been secreted away at first sight of McCurdle, there having been intimations of his interest in forcing a conversation he was certain needed to be had.

Fatefully, it was upon the Tecumsehs' next visit that McCurdle, after some two weeks of missed meetings, finally had the opportunity to encounter Grafton. Henslow was ill once again and Grafton was present well ahead of first pitch to oversee his boys. McCurdle arrived at the field to see his employer sitting in the front row of the otherwise empty grandstand, sumptuously dressed in a fine summer-weight suit and stiff Panama, leaning forward on his walking stick and talking to Lehmann, who stood on the field below.

Grafton waved and Lehmann turned and waved. McCurdle waved back and accelerated his pace, worried that the owner would find some excuse to beat a hurried retreat, but that did not come to pass. In fact it appeared that as McCurdle neared, Grafton politely ushered Lehmann away so as to ensure the confidentiality of their exchange.

Mick, said the owner, how are you this afternoon?

Well, Mr. Grafton, though not without some worry.

I expect I know what concerns you, but why don't you tell me?

Henslow, sir.

Of course.

He is not well.

Indeed not. Quite unwell. I'm aware, as I'm sure you know.

Respectfully I'd ask that you allow him to bow out and install someone new at the helm.

Mm. Any specific party you'd recommend, Mr. McCurdle?

Well, sir.

Yes.

I wonder if I might be given a shot. I'm known reputationally as a smart ballplayer, one who understands the game. And without risking immodesty I will say that I have had a hand in guiding the club recently, owing to old Henslow's trouble.

During our recent slide you mean, said Grafton with a small but wicked grin.

Well.

I'm only fooling you, McCurdle. And Grafton paused here, in what McCurdle felt was a moment wherein he was meant to consider Grafton's wealth, and his own place in the world, and the mechanisms inbuilt of the system that placed them where they sat and all but forbade their reversal. Are you perhaps, Grafton went on, interested in ensuring your place in the game once your playing days have concluded?

I don't know about that.

Because I understand such a time might be imminent given your body's state. Your arm specifically.

I've said nothing about my arm, Mr. Grafton.

You didn't need to. I have eyes. My own and others'.

I only want what's best for the club, sir.

I see. You may consider your petition filed, and it will be considered.

Thank you.

Now why don't you see about winning a game this afternoon. Might even help your cause.

McCurdle nodded and jogged away.

Thereafter he found himself in conference with Klopp, who McCurdle thought would also make a fine leader as it was generally catchers who best knew the game's hidden realities and arcane stratagems. Yes, if not me, thought McCurdle, then Long Tom should inherit this team.

Tom, said McCurdle, we're to be without Henslow again today.

I've heard it, Mick. I figured we'd submit the standard lineup again, assuming your arm's up to taking the box.

What the hell, sure.

Good, good.

They agreed then to confer on any matters requiring judgment during the contest, and as it happened, they were of the same mind when McCurdle coughed up six over the first two innings and had loaded them again in the third.

The old bigamist trotted out to the box and said, What do you say, Mick?

I'm done.

That was my sense but I owed it to you to ask. Should I wave Poppel in?

I think so. Then have Hewitt go tomorrow and give Poppel the Saturday slate.

My thinking too.

With McCurdle sitting the Pine Groves rallied late with big hits by Black, Lehmann, and Davis, and some sloppy fielding on the part of Tecumseh. In locking down the visitors' bats Hewitt flashed good accuracy and an ability to change speeds that caused McCurdle to wonder if he himself in his stubbornness and ambition had only been preventing Hewitt from developing to the fullness of his talents. Perhaps were it not for McCurdle's presence Hewitt and Poppel both would flourish the way an overshaded tree flares to sudden vigour when its larger neighbour falls. The sun beat down as he continued to entertain these thoughts, prompting him to drape a wet towel over his head until the final out was registered and the 9–6 victory for the Pine Groves recorded in the scorer's book.

The following morning, while McCurdle ate his oatmeal in the fashion he'd become accustomed to—that is, with his left hand, lifting the laden spoon past the front porcelain teeth so not to risk chipping his replacements—he read the game account in the *Recorder* as written by Welt and was shocked at information revealed therein.

Said the article, Those in the know anticipate an announcement imminently regarding Manager C. H. Henslow's declining health and the leadership of the Pine Groves club. The diamond squad's owner, Spencer T. Grafton, founder and proprietor of the Grafton Brewery, makers of Ashburnham's Famous Pine Grove Ale, is expected to disclose Mr. Henslow's immediate retirement followed by his own installation as field manager, and thereby to apply the acumen displayed by the success of his timber concern, by which he initially secured his fortune, and his beer business, which has propelled him into the financial stratosphere, to the game of base-ball. It is hoped by observers and partisans that the change will push the local nine "over the hump" in their effort to replace the Biltmore club of Guelph at the top of the league table.

Fuckery, said McCurdle.

He stopped eating, carried his bowl outside and left it beneath the step for the little cat, and then called on Klopp and Mrs. Klopp. And when the two players were sat in conference over coffee in the Klopps' small sitting room, Klopp said, I understand it's Grafton's plaything but if he's got any hope of success he ought to name someone with a base-ball mind to the role.

I wonder if you and I weren't being tried out these last few games with Henslow all but gone.

That might be. If so we did nothing to impress. But there could be some sense in talking to Grafton.

It seems clear his mind's made up, said McCurdle, clacking his false teeth with his tongue, a thing he'd begun doing and already done so often that he no longer knew when he was doing it.

If we lost a few more under him he might begin to doubt his own abilities, said Klopp, whose teeth remained all his own.

He might, but then we'd be sunk with no chance to catch Guelph and he'd have every excuse to clean house before next season.

It approached time for the players to report to the park and so their conspiratorial talk had to be shelved. En route they determined that Grafton approached the game as a dabbler or a hobbyist, but as he was doubly their employer they had no choice but to let the circumstances play themselves out and hope that Grafton might come to his senses. Each man silently resolved to himself that if that were to happen, he would be close at hand and ready to assume the onus of leadership.

There were then three fires burning in McCurdle's body that afternoon: first, Maureen; second, the red-hot discomfort in his shoulder and upper arm, extending into the elbow; and third, his unextinguished ambition, now fuelled by a desire to chasten Grafton, to show that he, McCurdle, still had penned horses set to be loosed. He said to Klopp, I've got to make an account of myself today, and Klopp understood.

In the clubhouse Grafton greeted the players as they filed in and said, Fine, fine, we're going to be fine here, gentlemen, over and over again.

McCurdle avoided an intimate conversation as long as he could but when he saw Grafton edge toward Henslow's office McCurdle stood and hurried after, worried the new field general was off to fill out the lineup. He caught Grafton just as he was going through the door.

Mr. Grafton.

McCurdle. It must be strange to see me in here and not old C. H., he said as he stepped behind Henslow's cherrywood desk.

It surely is.

I'll deliver a quick address to the men before we go out there, but I'll tell you now: don't worry about Henslow. I'll see that he's taken care of.

Where is he now?

At his home. I've hired a nurse to look in on him. And he'll be properly recognized here. He won't be swept under the rug. He's too important for that. We'll have a day in his honour, a band, bunting, speeches.

That will be quite a day, McCurdle said. He was not reassured on his dear leader's behalf, but even so he pressed through the topic and into the next one. Mr. Grafton, he said.

Call me by some less formal appellation. Boss or Skipper or Cap. Isn't that what you called Henslow?

Yes. Cap.

For captain.

Mr. Grafton, when Klopp and I were steering the ship yesterday in Henslow's absence and before we knew of your appointment, we'd intended on Hewitt going today.

Yes.

But I'd like to go instead.

You wish to pitch over Hewitt. For what reason?

I'd like to earn your confidence.

I'd like you to keep your arm together. You're no good to me in pieces.

My arm isn't important. I'll throw with my head, my heart, with a bloody stump. By Christ you let me start this game in the box and I'll bring it home for you.

Grafton's face suggested disinclination but then sensing McCurdle's desperation and also reasoning that public failure for McCurdle might prove advantageous for him (that is, Grafton) in any future negotiation, the rich man's eyes softened. I'd agree to that, he said, but I'd like it stipulated that it would be wise to consider your leash a short one.

I'd agree to that.

Then the ball is yours.

The two men stared at each other a long moment until it became understood to McCurdle that Grafton wanted him to leave. That was always how it was with the wealthy: they expected you to know when they were done with you and act on it yourself without them having to ask. McCurdle went off to dress.

Though all of the Pine Groves were aware to varying degrees of McCurdle's arm trouble only Klopp knew the true severity. In many ways their bond was concocted of trust and secret knowledge held tight. Each new secret was an investment in the brotherhood they shared. With all this understanding in place only a wordless nod in his catcher's direction was necessary to lure him into the equipment closet where, lit weakly by indirect sunlight through a single aperture, Klopp helped treat McCurdle's arm with cooling liniment and wrap it from neck to just below the elbow, all of which would be concealed by the heavy wool uniform once he took the field.

Have you anything for the pain? asked Klopp.

Just whisky. There's a fifth in my stall.

Go easy. Just as much as you need and not more or you won't be sharp. No morphine then.

Where the devil would I get Christing morphine, Kloppy? Damned if I know.

McCurdle draped his shirtless torso in a towel, Klopp opened the door, and they went back out into the clubhouse's main room. An aromatic delta of camphor and eucalyptus fumes trailed the fair-haired pitcher, who dressed as quickly as he could given the immobility of his shoulder.

The Tecumsehs were middling during that championship season, winning just as many as they lost and giving no strong indication of their character, be it that of a pitching team, a slugging team, a team built for speed, or one reliant on nifty defence. They generally allowed their opponent to dictate the tone of a given game and then reacted—or failed to. Their losses were deserved, their victories seemingly accidental.

There was an angry itch beneath McCurdle's swaddling, exacerbated by the tremendous heat. While sweat trickled down his back, he swung the arm in a wide slow circle hoping something bunched or twisted in there might loosen and relieve the burr. It didn't lessen, and he worked the whole game this way, with both searing pain and the distraction of this tingling, whatever its source.

He stood under the high sun in the very centre of the universe with three thousand pairs of eyes fixed on him and the interest of gamblers and teammates and Grafton, whose stake in McCurdle's performance was contradictory.

The first batter stood in: the Tecumsehs' second baseman, Lee, with an extravagant moustache and a shining red carbuncle beneath his right ear. The boil enticed McCurdle in that it looked like a target, but he fought the urge to see if he could burst it open with a high tight one because he did not care to start the game with a man on first. McCurdle reared back, lifted the ball in his hands over his head and grimaced, then fired a perfect strike that Lee never so much as saw.

Steeerike, judged old Feeney, and the game was underway.

The Tecumseh batsmen almost certainly failed to recognize the significance of the performance they were witnessing—to which they were indeed contributing by swinging impotently time and time again. McCurdle was held together by cotton stripping and paste, willing himself through agony and the rapid deterioration of several joints. He could both feel and hear them in fact, crunching and torquing and occasionally snapping like misplucked fiddle strings. The visitors eked out three base-hits across four innings but in each case the runner advanced no further than first before the side was retired and the Pine Groves were jogging in from the field, eager to take up their bats.

About which: Stroud led off by taking two balls and then rapping a lifeless bender to the deepest portion of left field. It slapped against the fence while he scurried around the bags, eventually standing on third with his uniform spotless for he'd been so fleet he'd had no need to slide. Tiny knocked him home on the first pitch he saw with a double, and then McCurdle muscled an inside ball over the first baseman's head. Tiny dove across home unnecessarily but the cloud of dust he raised was lovely to behold, bright and long suspended in the hot sun and windless air. McCurdle was on first with his left hand on his hip and a reaping hook buried in his right shoulder. The score stood at 3–0 before an out had been logged.

Then Davis stepped in. Upon his first swing it was apparent that he perceived there to be some account to settle, one supposes with Grafton, for Davis was a sensitive teammate with his ear to the ground and knew the chatter surrounding Grafton's takeover and likely overhaul of the roster. There was anger in his countenance and his posture, and he swung over the top of a dropper with such vehemence that he corkscrewed downward into the earth until reaching substrate. He finished off-balance and regretful, but not humbled, and he stood erect again twisting his hands on the bat's handle so forcefully it was as if he were strangling a viper. From first McCurdle thought he could hear the rasp and squeak of Davis's calloused hands rubbing against the rosin he'd shaken onto them and the dry woodgrain of the club.

The second pitch was high and Davis closed his eyes disdainfully and leaned slightly back as the ball sailed by, the catcher stretching to reach it. McCurdle took a step toward second but stopped and trotted back to the bag.

The Tecumseh pitcher was Big Bill Chesley, who stood six feet tall with an enormous head perched atop a frightfully robust chest and stomach, with legs like sequoias, and who was said to pack his valise with rocks to turn a simple trip into exercise for the legs, arms, and shoulders. His pitching delivery was violent and quick, his arm like a willow bough ratcheted backward and then released to whip forward in an uncontrolled manner, dispensing the ball so close to the batter's position that he felt he had no time to react to what was coming. Even when you got to Big Bill you felt you'd been lucky and mistakenly thrown your bat into the ball's path.

Davis, though, had Chesley's number, and had for years, going back to when he had come into the South Western from the Brantford Grands after the Southern Counties Fieldhands' Base-Ball League dissolved and its players were picked over. Davis had found himself with the Owen Sound club for one season before they themselves disbanded and he next latched on with the Maroons, where he remained for two campaigns. Big Bill had only ever toiled for the Tecumsehs, and from his first meeting with Davis he had found his heaviest and sneakiest deliveries no match for the slugger. Look around the game and you will find these sorts of relationships from time to time, and there would seem to be no explaining them. Davis feared Chesley not at all, and Bill's sole approach seemed to be to limit the damage, pitching away to Davis and giving him little to hit.

The third pitch of the meeting in question did not stray far enough from Davis's person. It hung just over the heart of the plate and with speed insufficient to vex the Groves' cleanup man. Davis planted his trailing foot, uncoiled his trunk, and met the ball just ahead of the plate with such a sound that a person would be forgiven for thinking that a shot had been fired or that the trunk of a great oak had snapped. Big Bill seemed to know the magnitude of the blast, for he did not turn to watch the ball race to its apex, only placed his hands on his hips and looked down and began with his feet to craft earthworks in the dirt of the pitcher's box.

The ballistic arc of the ball carried it high over the wall, and the trees situated just beyond, before it finally came to rest in a patch of milkweed on a rise above the riverbank. As it rolled there a frenzy of butterflies exploded heavenward. A groundskeeper was dispatched to retrieve the orb, and when it was found it was discovered to have lost its perfect rotundity, with the side struck by Davis having been flattened to a degree, and softened as well, such that for the remainder of the contest it flew with a slight bias and rolled in peculiar patterns, confounding hitters and fielders.

McCurdle was nearly run over because upon hearing the sound made by bat on ball, he'd simply stood upright and observed its majestic flight, even as Davis was coming up the first-base line at a steady though unhurried pace. After rounding the bag Davis was startled to find McCurdle still there, struck dumb and motionless.

Davis yelled, Hey, there, Mick, get along!

This prompted McCurdle to break into a jog while shouting over his shoulder, Christ sake, Josephus, you grazed the moon with that one.

The lead now standing at five to nil, it was possible for McCurdle to relent somewhat back in the pitching box, giving something less than his all on each and every individual throw. This he was grateful for, and in fact he came to understand that it would be the only way in which he might see the end of the game.

Even at reduced intensity, and with a five-run cushion, McCurdle sensed the razor edge he trod as his arm weakened, his fast one slowed, and his moving balls began to go flat. The Tecumseh second baseman, White, just missed one, getting a bit underneath it and sending it soaring into the high clear sky, where it seemed to hang up forever before settling into Stroud's hands. Chesley scorched one that was fortunately aimed right at Harry Black, who absorbed it with his gut and fell to his knees, cradling the ball for an out, while Big Bill cursed himself as he walked back to the bench.

The razor drew blood in the seventh when with one out Johnson, the Tecumseh catcher, drew a walk on four straight balls, and then Connaught, the shortstop, stood firm on a pitch that McCurdle failed to spin, taking it on the shoulder and making for two baserunners. White singled in Johnson and moved Connaught to third. Chesley came up and got all of McCurdle's drop ball, sending it over Tip's head before falling at the feet of Ab Cook who overran it by several paces and had to double back, allowing White and Connaught to come in and Chesley to arrive standing at second. That made the score 5–3 with still only one out recorded. Babcock then sacrificed Chesley to third before Bloom hit a looper that Lehmann couldn't squeeze, which allowed Chesley, though he'd been hanging back, to jog across the plate. Lehmann's throw into Davis then skipped through the second baseman's legs and all the way to Tiny, who picked it up to try to nab Bloom at second but ended up sailing a wild toss back into right allowing Bloom to stand up from his slide and bolt for third. Lehmann rushed in toward the infield and scooped up the ball a second time. He thought he had the momentum to make the throw to third, where Stroud was now covering, but in fact he had too much momentum and his throw found its way into the grandstand seats, where men fought over it. Bloom meanwhile stepped across home to tie the game.

Grafton's pomaded hair came unglued and his celluloid collar worked loose from all the screaming and gesticulating he'd been doing since the inning had started to unravel with one out. Hell's bells, McCurdle, just get one Christing out, he shouted. One fucking out!

A moment later McCurdle, amid a rather grotesque popping sensation, released a slow blooper pitch that rose high and then descended across the plate. Fitts, the Tecumseh right fielder, grew impatient waiting for it to fall into his hitting zone, his eyes widening and his tongue protruding. When it finally neared he lunged and his hands rolled over, causing him to land only a glancing blow on the top of the ball, sending it weakly downward toward the box. McCurdle took three steps, fielding it where it rested in the small cloud of dust it had kicked up, and lobbed a throw to Black for the third out while Fitts stood holding his bat and glowering at McCurdle.

When McCurdle reached the bench Grafton was standing with his jacket open, his thumbs hitched in his belt, and his chest puffed comically. McCurdle, he barked, what the hell was that?

They got to me. I'll buckle down. Let's get the lumber going, he shouted to his teammates.

Easy, said Grafton, why don't you sit and I'll get a fresh arm going next inning. Poppel, you'll go in.

Like hell, said McCurdle.

I'm sorry?

The bench went quiet, the usual hubbub silenced. Lehmann had been passing around a pouch of chaw, Stroud lighting a slender cigarillo, and Davis taking a deep draught on a water pail followed by a nip of rye from the flask he kept tucked in his back pocket, but all activity ceased when McCurdle issued his refusal. Eyes began to dart furtively as each man sought confirmation from another that he'd heard what he thought he'd just heard.

The Christing hell I'll sit down, Grafton. I'm going to finish what I started. You'll have to pin me down and tie me up or knock me all the way out to stop me. If that contravenes your designs I apologize, but I won't yield.

McCurdle, you're going to talk yourself out of a job.

We can discuss my future on this club and your brewery after this game ends, but frankly you wouldn't know how to make a base-ball decision if your life depended on it. You ought to have handed the club to someone with some experience instead of assuming that your money granted you some kind of knowledge. It grants you fuck all in this arena.

Klopp, who was busy inserting a cord of shredded tobacco into the pocket of his lower lip, gave a quick and involuntary chuckle at this before fraudulently coughing to cover it, as he didn't particularly wish to spend the winter hunting for another ballclub to catch for when the snow melted again.

Is that so, sniffed Grafton. Well this is my ballclub, and you're my ballplayer, and I say you're done for the day. You've done enough damage. Sit down and shut your maw and maybe I'll be able to forget this impudence if we should miraculously rally to win this game.

McCurdle was sitting now at the end of the bench and staring ahead at the field, where the Tecumseh pitcher had retaken the box and was throwing to loosen his arm before Black took his turn at the dish to start the bottom of the inning.

I'll be back out there in three outs' time, he said quietly. You're welcome to try to stop me, Grafton.

Unsettled perhaps by the conflict on the bench and the dissent among their ranks that it belied, the Pine Groves mounted no rally but went quietly in order by strikeout, ground out, and fly ball. Thereafter McCurdle did not await instruction but simply trotted out to the box and picked up the ball which had been rolled there by the Tecumseh fielder who'd caught the last out. Klopp took his spot behind the dish and waited for McCurdle to send in a few warmup tosses. He expected at any moment to see Grafton storm out onto the field spouting epithets and surly philippics, but when Long Tom ventured a glance over toward the bench he saw his new manager only fuming in silence, arms folded tight, pacing the length of the bench, perhaps a new redness to his face.

It would have been poetically just if the next events had been draped in glory, and if McCurdle's performance that inning had proved to be one for the ages, but it would come to appear that no muse, no deity, nor guiding spirit visited upon the Quaker Grounds that afternoon. McCurdle's right arm had simply met the last of its strike-throwing mastery. It was now just a wet noodle electrified to deliver shocks to his nerves with each motion. He walked the first batter on four sloppy tosses, then clipped the second hitter on the elbow. In trying to throw his trick ball to the third he could generate no spin and so it hung out there, tempting and undeceiving, for the striker to club it. In a rare stroke of luck it was lashed directly at Tiny for the out, but both baserunners had held up and each scampered safely back to his bag. So there was one out but men at first and second, and Chesley was due up.

There seethed within McCurdle's chest a glowing hatred and a will to overcome his body's disintegration, but the failings promising his misfortune were physical in nature and could not be surmounted by spirit alone. For the briefest of moments he allowed himself to think of Maureen, of the peace he might soon know resting his head on her breast and closing his eyes in an act of longed-for capitulation. Then he looked around at the men who counted on him and who would be in for a hell of a fight if they were to get back to the top of the South Western heap and earn their spot against the goddamned horsefucking Biltmores in that final series. What McCurdle couldn't quite determine was whether what he owed these men—Kloppy and Black, Lehmann, old Josephus, and the rest of them, and poor dead Keenan, and dear, dear Henslow—was one last dauntless act of courage and skill, or the good sense to step out of the way and allow them to guide their own ship.

With the count at one ball and one strike and Chesley practically salivating over McCurdle's reduced velocity, McCurdle lobbed a cookie at the plate and Chesley, it might be fairly said, was only too happy to partake. One observer later mused that the struck ball reached such an altitude that when it came down—far, far beyond the wall in left centre—it was rimed with frost. Chesley slow-jogged his circumnavigation of the bases and all present knew that the lowly Tecumsehs had just put the game out of reach. When the beaten and softened ball was at last returned to McCurdle he was all but booking his train ticket to Brockville.

On the bench Grafton had taken a seat, leaning slightly back with his arms folded against his chest and a look on his face at once betraying both utter fury and giddy vindication. All a person wanted to know about Grafton's plan moving forward could be gleaned from the pose of his body and the set of his face. He had already accepted the loss of this game, and was mapping out the rest of the season.

Somehow, through guile or more likely through the heroic efforts of his fielders, McCurdle found his way to the end of the frame with two more baserunners but no additional runs across. He sauntered off the field dreading the next moment, but Grafton said nothing, and did not so much as peek in McCurdle's direction.

Again the Pine Groves failed to score in their chance at the plate, and when it was time to take the field again Grafton simply said, Poppel, go on out there and finish it.

The men all knew everything implied therein, with Cook taking centre and McCurdle done for the day if not for good. The game ended as expected—with a loss—and Grafton offered no words of encouragement to his depleted squad. They dressed and dispersed in mute indignity.

McCurdle never again saw his name in pencil in the starting lineup for the Ashburnham Pine Groves, or indeed any other ballclub, but knew only spot action in the outfield late in games already decided in one way or the other. The Groves, with a sudden alteration in their essential character, did not manage to overtake the Biltmores as August wore on, but slipped further back as they appeared listlessly to accept their fate. On several mornings in late August the residents of Ashburnham awoke to a chill which portended the coming change of season and so, with no thrilling pennant race to occupy them, their thoughts turned to preparations for winter and the necessary business of survival. The crowds at the Quaker Grounds thinned noticeably as the apples reddened.

The first of September came and the Biltmores were kings of the second half, their supremacy unchallenged. A parade was planned through the streets of Guelph, McCurdle read in the *Recorder.* He knew what came next and gave some thought to jumping town in order to sidestep it, but in the end decided to let things take their course. He stayed on over the weekend and on Monday morning, upon reaching the grainhouse, he was dismissed by Fuller, the foreman, who displayed no emotion in reporting the news.

McCurdle began drinking immediately. He downed a succession of ales at Potter's and then procured three bottles of rye whisky which were done before the sun went down. Then he careened about Ashburnham on something like a farewell tour, encountering patrons and proprietors alike who, when they recognized him, offered to pay for his refreshments. He took them up on these offers, and by midnight he no longer resembled a civilized human being. He slept an hour beneath a clump of bent-over cattails with his left hand in the river and his right folded onto his chest as though half set for funereal rites, only to startle awake when an owl called. Then McCurdle was off again, wandering nowhere and everywhere, kicking over flowerpots and urinating on the clubhouse door.

He boarded the train at two the following afternoon with no notion of where he'd spent most of the preceding daylight hours, though he did recall being in his room briefly—just long enough to register a telegram that had been slipped under his door, which he assumed to be further chastisement from Grafton, and to pack a small trunk with the few items he wished to carry forward into his new life: a hat, two good shirts, his mother's bible, six pairs of socks, and so forth. His porcelain teeth sat delicate upon a saucer. He was certain he'd had them in for most of his bar-room visits the night before but then recalled waking up by the river without them and so reasoned that at some point now quite lost to him he must have returned to the room with the specific intent of removing his dental plate and placing it on a white bone-china dish.

With his smile in place though not on display he stood on the platform and before stepping up onto the train, he turned and offered whatever might be the opposite of a benediction to the town of Ashburnham. He extended his left hand over his head not in a wave but as if in the placement of a hex, but since he had no belief in such things it was only a gesture of dismissal cast over a broad area—though if it could be said to have a point of concentration it would have been the brewery, more specifically the office of Spencer Thomas Grafton.

McCurdle hammered southward out of town with his head set to burst and his mouth full of gravel. He registered the date of his termination as the sudden dissolution of several important aspects of his life, as well as a coming apart of much of what he'd valued within himself. He'd known there would be an end to these days but figured on being more the author of the decisive moment than the subject.

After changing trains at Toronto, McCurdle sat at a window observing as Lake Ontario lay unmoved while he sped east along its northern shore toward Brockville. He could not have been aware that he was also racing towards the sad news of the schoolhouse being gone, and Maureen with it.

The school's electric heater, used against the early-morning first-of-September chill, had sparked and caught, and then a curtain had taken light followed by the wall-boards and the ceiling, and then the whole little building was engulfed, claiming her and two children as well. The head of the fire brigade later reported that Maureen had had the children in her arms when their lives were choked out of them and just before they were consumed by the flames. She was remarkable to the end. Of course she was.

The sad tale had been told in a letter penned by Mrs. Morgan, the tea house owner who'd known Maureen and McCurdle and been aware of their connection. She'd hoped he might be made aware of the tragedy from someone he knew and not from the pages of a newspaper, and it was she who'd authored the telegram that had been slipped under McCurdle's door that morning, which he had failed to read.

The horrifying news would instead find him the following day in the form of a comment from an old acquaintance suggesting he must have returned to Brockville to bury Maureen. McCurdle asked, Why would I bury her? and upon learning it was like a thousand fastballs to the mouth, leaving him staggered forever thereafter, as hollowed out by her death as he'd been by her absence when she was alive.

After days of silence and blackness he would emerge and prove instrumental in the effort to rebuild the schoolhouse. He would subsequently be offered custodial duties thereof, which he would accept. As a constant benign presence he would remain there for many years, a bachelor whose only joy was to teach the boys to play base-ball, and some of the girls.

And in the blink of an eye he would be hurtled into a century he could not recognize nor understand, loud and smog-choked and astounding. He would be past his era, and all he held most dear would have slipped by the wayside. By the time of his death he would have seen no more of the world but a great deal of base-ball, though he would never in his life witness a major-league contest. Someone would ask if he wished to and he would reply that perhaps he would but as it was unlikely that a big-league club would establish itself in Brockville, Ontario, his opportunity would almost certainly never come.

Lassitude would seep in, and his shoulders would drop and his belt expand. The ghosts of old base-ball injuries would haunt his joints. He would not be able to lift his right arm above the shoulder, and pain would yet zap erratically from his elbow to the tip of his little finger.

Quite near his death, but not so near that he could sense its imminence, while sitting one late summer day on the selfsame bench he'd occupied with Maureen many years previous and watching the river slide by, bound eastward for the cataracts at Long Sault and through Quebec and distantly spilling out into the churning Atlantic, he would gain a scintilla of the clarity that had so long eluded him.

It would occur to him quite suddenly, the thoughts rushing in unbidden to fill his brain as though something had tapped his skull and begun pumping them in. He'd say to himself that he had lived alongside and played with men who'd lived lives rich in sorrow and regret, who were too careless in their language, too quick with their fists. Wounded men, acting—driving forward, consuming, in turn wounding—while ignorant of the fact of their own wounding. He would understand too his own losses as the source of his residual sorrow: his mother's death and the curtain between them while she held on, and his inability to comfort her as well as her inability to comfort him. His father's barbarousness, which had in turn been planted in him, and by his own rude beginning, thrust out into the slavering bloodthirsty world too soon, too bare. Maureen's death, and the life he'd foolishly forestalled while she was alive. His own need for forgiveness, given and received. All of it. The whole ballgame.

He would see with more clarity a system which required men to lash out in fear and desperation, to work their fingernails to the quick simply to eat and clothe themselves, and to react with rancour and bloodshed when their place in this system was threatened. He'd see it was this system that meant he'd never seen his brother again, a system cosmically unnecessary—all of it completely unneeded—but so compelling in its dishonesty and so pervasive it assumed the weight of natural law. He would intuit too how all this explained his lifelong anger toward his fellow men, with but a few exceptions, because he'd needed someone to blame for this faceless cruelty and those men were decent scapegoats and close at hand.

But none of that would come for several years. In the meantime he was in a Grand Trunk passenger car on a weekday with his hat resting on his lap, heading toward news that would change him irrevocably but which could not find him along the way. He had to move to it. Of course it is not that way now, but that's how it was in Robert James McCurdle's time.

# ACKNOWLEDGEMENTS

The author wishes to express gratitude to the Ontario Arts Council for the very generous Literary Creation grant which enabled the production of this work.

The author also wishes to thank the estimable Mr. William Humber, teacher and historian, for undertaking an early read of this manuscript in order to ascertain the plausibility of the fictional events depicted herein.

The author further extends a hand of recognition toward Norm Nehmetallah, publisher, for so quickly and so enthusiastically endorsing this project and seeing it through to completion.

The author remains in the considerable debt of Bryan Ibeas, editor, who continues to improve, refine, and champion the author's work.

The preceding work would not have been possible without the presence of an untold number of harmless arachnids who took up residence in a certain treehouse situated in the forest abutting the far eastern end of a certain lake in central Ontario, and whose presence frightened and repulsed the author's children, thereby placing the treehouse in said children's disfavour, thus allowing the author to take it up as a space of work, wherein much of the writing of this book was undertaken during the early summer of 2023.

Lastly and most importantly the author offers grateful words to his wife, Christie, words far too enfeebled beneath the task of expressing his admiration and love for her, but those words being all he has to offer, finally, alongside his promise to keep striving to one day be worthy of her colossal patience.

**Andrew Forbes** is the author of the story collections *Lands and Forests* (2019) and *What You Need* (2015), which was shortlisted for the Danuta Gleed Literary Award, and named a finalist for the Trillium Book Prize. His first novel, *The Diapause*, will be released in late 2024. He is also the author of two collections of baseball writing, *The Utility of Boredom* and *The Only Way is the Steady Way*. His work has appeared in publications such as the *Toronto Star, Canadian Notes and Queries,* and *Maisonneuve Magazine*. Born in Ottawa, Forbes has lived in Atlantic Canada and rural eastern Ontario, and now resides in Peterborough, Ontario.

Invisible Publishing produces fine Canadian literature for those who enjoy such things. As an independent, not-for-profit publisher, we work to build communities that sustain and encourage engaging, literary, and current writing.

Invisible Publishing has been in operation for over a decade. We released our first fiction titles in the spring of 2007, and our catalogue has come to include works of graphic fiction and nonfiction, pop culture biographies, experimental poetry, and prose.

We are committed to publishing writers with diverse perspectives. In acknowledging historical and systemic barriers, and the limits of our existing catalogue, we emphatically encourage writers from LGBTQ2SIA+ communities, Indigenous writers, and writers of colour to submit their work.

Invisible Publishing is also home to the Bibliophonic series of music books and the Throwback series of CanLit reissues.

If you'd like to know more, please get in touch: info@invisiblepublishing.com